Also by Linda Jordan:

Notes on the Moon People
  Falling Into Flight
  Bibi's Bargain Boutique
  Living in the Lower Chakras
  Faerie Unraveled: Bone of the Earth Book 1

Come on over to Linda's website and join the fun!
  www.LindaJordan.net

Don't miss a release!
  Sign up for Linda's Serendipitous Newsletter while you're there.

Writers love reviews, even short, simple ones. Please go to where you bought this book from or Goodreads and leave a review. It would be much appreciated.

HORTICULTURAL HOMICIDE

Published by Metamorphosis Press

www.MetamorphosisPress.com

Copyright 2017 by Linda Jordan

All rights reserved

ISBN-13: 9780997797152

This is a work of fiction. Names, characters, places or incidents are either the product of the author's imagination or are used fictitiously. Any resemblance to actual events, or persons, either living or dead, is entirely coincidental.

HORTICULTURAL HOMICIDE

※

LINDA JORDAN

For Michael & Zoe

DAY 1 - FRIDAY

Georgina Wetherby, Gina, stared out the large picture window facing Puget Sound, debating whether to wear a raincoat or fleece. Rain. It looked like rain. Down below, whitecaps were picking up. She could see spray from a gray whale's blow. They were just offshore, feeding on shrimp.

Her small house sat perched on a hillside overlooking the Sound. A chunk of generous acreage which was mostly flat. The hill, above and below, was stable. Unlike many in this part of the country. Ewan had seen to that. He'd had every type of survey done to ensure the craftsman style house was safe before they'd bought it decades ago. As a summer house.

Gina had fallen in love with it at first sight. Weary of maintaining the huge three story house on Capital Hill in Seattle, this one was perfect. One story, four bedrooms, which was perfect for them. His office, her studio, a guest room and their bedroom.

Now of course, it was too much for just her. She was on her own now.

Ewan had retired from lawyering for nonprofits at sixty, she'd left her marketing job and they'd moved out here to Raven

Island. Sold the house in Seattle, where the kids had grown up. Then he'd had several strokes over just a few months and died.

He'd up and died on her.

Gina picked up her mug of tea from the thick oak table and sipped the now cold liquid.

She'd been alone for five years.

Alone except for Albert and Alice, her monster Maine Coon cats, who she'd gotten from the local animal shelter as kittens. Albert was perched on the back of the couch, bathing his luxurious black fur with gray tips, and occasionally chirping at birds outside in the garden. Alice had stolen Gina's favorite chair. The orange and white puff of fur curled in a circle so one couldn't see her face or her tail, looking for all the world like a fuzzy pillow.

Gina downed the rest of the rose congou tea and cream, savoring the richness, then rinsed the mug and put it in the dishwasher. Then glanced at the clock. 8 a.m.

She'd better get going. Those illustrations weren't going to paint themselves. The May Day Show at the gallery was coming up fast and she wasn't going to get caught empty-handed.

Gina slid the forest green raincoat over her long sleeve blue T-shirt and jeans, then decided on rubber boots in case she wanted to walk in the nursery's garden. She glanced at the mirror and tried to pat her short-cropped silver hair down, then gave up. She picked up her art supplies, water bottle, purse and keys. As an afterthought, she grabbed her canvas rain hat.

"See you later kids, be good."

Then closed and locked the door that led to the carport. She loaded up the sky blue Prius and got in.

It only took five minutes to get to Ravenswood Nursery. Five minutes of two lane blacktop weaving through massive cedars, Douglas firs and big leaf maples. The latter which hung heavy with blooms and tiny leaves which would grow to be larger than her head.

It was still early April, but it felt springlike. The air full of the hope of new growth.

There were several cars in the gravel parking lot already. Staff getting ready for a big day.

This week a big horticultural conference had been held in Seattle. Today, Saturday, Sunday and Monday were tours of local gardens. The nursery was on the tour maps.

People from all over the world would be coming to the nursery hoping to score rare and exotic plants. Delia Swanson, one of the owners, traveled extensively hunting plants. Climbing up mountainsides and bringing back seeds and cuttings. Propagating rare beauties and selling them. Introducing them to American gardeners. She wrote books about her travels and the plants. She was a rising star in the Horticultural firmament.

Over the years, Gina had watched Delia build a mystique around the nursery's brand. She admired her business instincts, but Delia was a workaholic and a bit of a braggart. "I've got this plant and you don't."

The nursery did mail order, as well as in-person sales. The website was a wonder to behold. The place had become so popular they sold out of plants faster than they could propagate them. If you wanted something, you needed to order early.

One of her closest friends, Melanie Caruthers, worked at the nursery as the propagation manager, so Gina heard a lot about the place. The good and the bad. Melanie was also the one who'd gotten permission for Gina to come in and do her work at the nursery.

She parked in a tiny spot, out of the way of guests, and got her supplies out of the back seat, leaving the purse and hat. Gina locked the car and headed off for the tropical greenhouse.

The nursery lay on ten acres, seven of which held a world class garden, the other three acres contained greenhouses, a small store, a tented seating area for customers to eat brown bag lunches or just sit, and Delia and Renee's house.

Gina walked down the gravel path littered with lavender flowers dropped by the majestic empress tree. The tubular blossoms, the size of a finger, gave off a sweet scent that perfumed the air all the way past the first set of greenhouses. She walked down the gravel aisle, a greenhouse on every side. These were hoop houses, long tunnels of heavy clear plastic, held up by arches of pipe. Flat walls with doors enclosed each end.

Delia popped out of a greenhouse followed by Max, her black dog who looked part lab, part Australian shepherd. He ran over to Gina and wagged his tail.

"Well, good morning Max. How ya doin'?" Gina asked, ruffling his soft fur.

"Hi Gina. Are you painting today?"

"Yes, I thought I'd work in the tropical greenhouse. Try to stay out of the shoppers' way." There was nothing for sale in that greenhouse.

"Wonderful. I know people will love to see you at work," said Delia, smiling. "Oh, check and see if Maisie's in there, would you? She didn't come for breakfast. Of course, she might have caught something to eat. She was out all hunting all night."

Delia was dressed in her normal khaki pants, rubber boots, t-shirt and Ravenswood Nursery hoodie. Her curly strawberry blond hair was loose instead of tied back, which meant she was dressed up. For leading tours, not gardening.

"I'll look for her," said Gina. "Good luck with the tours."

"I just love showing off the nursery and gardens. This conference is going to cement our place on the map."

"Bye Max," said Gina.

He barked in reply, then followed Delia off down the gravel path, bouncing like a puppy and quickly overtaking her long strides.

Gina continued in the opposite direction.

Everything in the world revolved around Delia and her

nursery. At least as far as Delia was concerned. Little else interested her.

The farthest pair of greenhouses inside the area not roped off, were heated. They were both marked private. The one on the left was the first propagation greenhouse, where babies were being grown on before they moved into the sale greenhouses. The one on the right was the tropical greenhouse. Display plants and some of Delia's personal collection lived here during the winter.

Gina walked in the door, shutting it behind her. The warmth and humidity were obvious. And the scent was incredible. There was a jasmine or maybe a Gardenia, or both, blooming now. She hadn't paid attention because she was focused on splashy flowers for this show. Normally, she looked at foliage. But with the May Day theme, lush flowers seemed more appropriate.

Several large plants were missing from the front of the greenhouse. It must have been deemed safe to take them outside for the day. Or perhaps they'd been moved out until fall. Gina didn't pay much attention to tropical plant needs. She just liked to paint them, not grow them.

She walked down the aisle to where she'd been working yesterday. Her stool was still there. She set her bag of supplies down on a plywood plant table and slipped out of her raincoat, putting it next to the bag. She walked through the greenhouse, looking at the plant benches. On the one closest to the portable heater, she found Maisie, curled up in a black ball.

"Hi Maisie, do you want out?" Gina petted her sleek fur.

Maisie lifted her head, opened her golden eyes, meowed and curled back up to sleep.

"Well, I guess not."

The nursery cats, Maisie and Flopsy, had long ago found any holes in the greenhouses' plastic and came and went at will. They probably preferred the heated greenhouses, as did mice or other wildlife.

She extracted her folding easel from the bag and set it up.

Then pulled out the watercolor pad with her partially finished painting on it. Then her paints, brushes, paint-water cup and bottle. She set the paints and brushes on the plant bench. Opened the water bottle and poured some water into the cup and set it on the easel as well. Then sipped cold water from the bottle and put it on the plant bench.

Gina was painting a lavender and peach-colored Hibiscus with swirly petals. It was a lovely thing. It might be marginally hardy here, in the ground. But it certainly wouldn't be blooming in April, if it was outside.

She heard two women talking outside the comfortable bubble of the tropical greenhouse, but couldn't hear the actual words. There were shadows on the gravel path outside.

Then the voices grew louder. Delia and Renee, Delia's partner in business and love.

"You lying bitch! You said there was nothing between the two of you. Then I heard last night that you slept with him," yelled Renee.

"Renee, it was nothing really. I just wanted to try him out."

"For what? Are you auditioning him? To replace me?"

"No. I love you," yelled Delia.

"If you loved me, you wouldn't be sleeping around."

The arguing continued. It made Gina uncomfortable, hearing such personal information. Yet, she couldn't stop listening.

"We can work this out," said Delia. "I know it."

"What if I don't want to work it out? What if I don't want to share you? And now you want to bring him into the business?"

"He's got a lot of money. It would help so much."

"I don't want his bloody money!" yelled Renee. "Besides we have an offer from one of the drug companies."

"Yes, but it's not enough. We'll need more money than that to do everything we want."

"Well, I don't want him in the business."

"We'll talk about this later. There's too many people around."

"No, we won't talk about this later. This discussion is closed!" yelled Renee.

Even through the muffling plastic wall, Gina heard her stomp off on the crunchy gravel path.

Wow, that was a lot of information she didn't want to know. Delia sleeping with a man. Renee and Delia had just celebrated their fifteenth anniversary as a couple. Then about ten years ago, they'd become business partners and opened the nursery. Now Delia was sleeping around with some man who wanted to buy into the business? Who could that be? She was sure lots of people would want to join the partnership, but not many of them had money. The nursery was having more than its fifteen minutes of fame right now.

Gina shook her head to clear it and refocused her attention. She worked steadily for an hour, laying down layer after layer of color near the center of the flowers, deepening the leaves' shadows. Making the painting more accurate with each stroke. She'd done the wash of the plant yesterday. Today was detail work. Precision was important for botanical illustrations.

The door opened and Melanie stuck her head in. She wore the Ravenswood hoodie, and probably under that the Ravenswood Nursery t-shirt, jeans and running shoes. Melanie always wore those. Her short-cropped hair was silver, just like Gina's. They were the same age, birthdays just a few weeks apart. Gina had only lived on the island a few weeks before they met and became friends. After Ewan died, they'd become fast friends. Melanie had saved her life, dragging her out of the house and back into the world.

"Oh hi, Gina. Have you seen Delia?"

"When I first got here. About an hour ago. She was heading that way," Gina said, pointing.

"Okay, I'll be taking a break in a while and come see you."

"I'll be here."

Melanie disappeared and closed the door.

Renee came in with a troop of fifteen people.

"This is our tropical greenhouse," she said. "Here are all the lovely things we just can't live without here in the Northwest, but we have to keep them heated all winter in order to make them happy. Some of our tropicals have already been making their way outside."

Renee was the Marketing Director for the business. Gina quite liked her, having been in marketing for a small retail chain in Seattle meant they spoke the same language. Still, Gina was surprised to see her out here giving a tour to Hort Heads. This was Delia's domain. And if not Delia, then Karen, the nursery manager, or one of the more knowledgable staff. Plant geeks always had plant questions.

"And this is Gina Weatherby. She's a famous botanical illustrator and artist who comes by now and again to paint. Her work is in great demand."

"Good morning," said Gina, waving and silently thanking Renee for the great promo.

"What are you working on?" asked Renee.

"I thought I'd try and capture this lovely Hibiscus while it's in bloom. The flower colors are so beautiful."

People gathered round as best they could and asked questions about painting, plant choices for illustrations and all sorts of things. Gina happily answered them. Renee looked slightly relieved.

Once Melanie stuck her head in. Renee glanced at her and shook her head. Melanie left.

Gina wondered what their communication meant.

The group moved on to another greenhouse. Gina had to admire Renee's ability to calm herself, or partition her hurt away. After that argument, she wouldn't have been able to do it.

She heard Max barking, which was strange. He rarely barked.

Her paint water was dirty again. She poured it out onto the gravel beneath the plant table. Then went to pour from her water bottle. It was empty. This was the fifth time she'd changed the water. Her bottle only held four water changes.

The closest place for water was the mist greenhouse. Gina took the bottle and went outside. She ducked under the yellow cord that meant 'Do not go here — this is really, really private.' It was meant to keep customers away from the more sensitive propagation greenhouses.

There were four greenhouses here, all heated, some more than others. Three were filled with what looked like twigs or the teensiest of plants. These were brand new babies. Most were barely a season old and it would be a year, or two, before they were salable.

Max was outside the fourth greenhouse, still barking and pawing at the door.

The fourth greenhouse was a combination of Delia's secret stash of rare plants and the mist room. The mist room was separated from the rest of the greenhouse by a wall of plastic, and was almost continuously misted, providing the humidity needed to root cuttings of plants.

It was far from the other greenhouses, so there would be fewer people going in and out. The high humidity, and freedom from disease were important.

"What's up buddy?" she asked, petting him. He kept barking frantically.

Gina opened the door. Max raced in. She slipped in, closing the door. This half of the greenhouse was a bit cooler than the tropical one, but still warm. It was filled with rare plants, beautiful and ugly. Delia had been collecting plants for decades. Some got propagated and did well out in the gardens. Others couldn't survive out there or were simply too choice, and were kept in here.

Gina followed Max to the mist room where the faucet was. He barked and she opened the door and slid in quickly. Walking down the aisle, water misting her from above. Here the small pots or flats looked like bare soil with sticks in them. Table after table of them.

She followed Max down the aisle towards the faucet. He stopped between two tables, near a dark form on the ground.

She stopped. Delia lay there on her side, facing away from Gina.

"Are you okay?" she asked.

There was no answer. Max was licking Delia's ear and whining.

Gina knelt down and jiggled her by the shoulder.

She rolled Delia over and saw a huge gash on her head.

Delia didn't respond. Gina touched Delia's cheek, which felt cold. But then again, she'd been lying on the ground.

Call 911. She patted her jeans pocket, but no. She'd left her phone in the bag with her art supplies.

Then beneath the plant bench Gina saw a bloody shovel.

She ran for the tropical greenhouse. She dropped her water bottle on the plant bench and dug for her phone.

Gina called 911 and gave directions, hoping the ambulance would arrive first.

Then she called Melanie.

"Ravenswood Nursery, Melanie here."

"Mel, I found Delia. She's hurt. In the mist room. I called 911. Make sure there's someone out front to meet them."

"Gina?"

"Yes. Did you hear me?"

"I'll do it. Where are you?"

"On my way back to the mist tent. I had to go get my phone. Also tell Renee."

"I'll do that and then meet you there."

Gina was rushing back to the mist greenhouse.

Inside, she stood there, talking to Delia. Max lay in the aisle beside Delia, licking Delia's hand and whining.

"Delia, can you hear me? I'm getting help. The ambulance will be here soon."

She was joined shortly by Melanie.

"I told Renee. She's trying to find someone to take over her tour group. We're short-handed today."

"Is someone out front?"

"I sent Tyler out."

"Delia looks so pale."

"Should we move her?" asked Melanie.

"I don't think so. The ambulance and police will be here soon. If she's broken something we could screw it up worse."

Renee came rushing in. Melanie and Gina moved aside. Max didn't, he just lay facing Delia and looking mournful, head on his paws.

"Delia, honey. Are you okay? What happened? Delia, please be all right." Renee was on her hands and knees beside Delia. Then she said, "I'm so sorry."

What did that mean? Sorry for the argument? Or had Renee hit her with the shovel?

What a mean thought. Of course Renee hadn't hit Delia.

The wail of a siren rose in the distance and came closer.

"I'll wait outside," said Gina.

She left the mist tent and then the greenhouse.

Outside it was cooler, but the day was turning out to be warm for April. Maybe it would even hit sixty degrees. Gina stared down the path, looking for the medics. When she saw them she waved madly.

She held the yellow rope up so the man and woman could duck under easier and then opened the greenhouse door and pointed.

"Back through the second door." Which she noticed was open. Delia would be angry, if she was conscious.

Gina followed the medics, shutting both doors behind her.

Renee scrambled out of their way, tears streaming down her

face. Melanie grabbed Max's collar and said, "Max, come." She led him away from Delia.

The medics got down and examined her.

Finally, they looked at each other. Then the woman said, "I'm afraid she's dead."

Renee said, "No, you must be wrong. She can't be dead."

Melanie gasped.

Gina felt the knot in the pit of her stomach grow larger.

How could Delia be dead? She'd just seen her alive.

One of the medics was on the phone.

Melanie was wiping tears off her face.

"I should go back out. More people will be arriving. Should we close the nursery?" Melanie asked Renee.

Renee looked at Melanie, as if grasping the question and all it implied. She sat down on the hard gravel behind the medics and stared at Delia. Max got up and crawled into her lap, his large body blanketing hers. Renee hugged him and buried her face in his coat.

Melanie looked at Gina, questioningly.

Then Renee looked up and said, "No. We shouldn't close the nursery. That's the last thing Delia would have wanted."

"Okay then," said Gina to Melanie. "Let's go out and pitch in."

Melanie nodded.

They left the greenhouse, shutting the doors behind. The Raven Island Sheriff was coming down the gravel path, Tyler leading him. Tyler was one of the young men who worked at the nursery. He was young, maybe nineteen. The muscle, was what Melanie called the two men. They always got the heavy jobs. He looked relieved to see Melanie, and ran back towards the front. It must be busy. He was probably carrying people's plants to their cars today.

Gina led the Sheriff to the greenhouse, opened the door and said, "Through the plastic door, halfway down. Should we close the nursery?"

He said, "Let me see what we're dealing with first. Just keep everybody out of this section."

She knew they'd be talking later.

Gina caught up with Melanie.

"Should we tell people that Delia's dead?"

Melanie said, "I don't know. People will be asking where she is. Maybe we can just say we don't know. At least to most of them."

"That'll work. One person is hard to pin down on ten acres. If we're in the garden, then she's in the greenhouses somewhere and vice versa."

She'd feel guilty for lying, but that was better than telling people that Delia had been murdered. By someone unknown. She shivered.

Gina spent most of the day helping people find plants in the nursery, trying not to think about Delia's bashed in head and the person who might have done it. Melanie, Karen and Brianna were leading garden tours. Brianna had been pulled from filling mail orders. Stacy was at the cash register in the store. Tyler on carry-out. David had called in sick that day, stomach flu he said. What a day to miss work.

And of course they'd planned on having Delia and Renee there to help out. Eight people would have been perfect. Six were not, especially since Gina didn't really know that much about where the plants were and what they needed to live happily. Good thing Delia had printed out a catalog for the greenhouses with locations about which plants were in what greenhouse.

Gina saw Renee and Max go toward the house. It took a long, long time before the medics took Delia's body away. Three more deputies, or maybe sheriffs, had arrived since then.

The hardest part was answering people's questions.

"One of the nursery staff died. They're investigating. That's what they do if it's not clear the person had an illness or heart attack or whatever," was her standard answer.

She felt dishonest.

Even though it was not anyone's business, Gina knew all of them would have cared. The various horticultural communities were small and they overlapped. Most everyone had heard of Ravenswood and Delia.

During a lull between carloads of customers, Gina grabbed a water and a pulled-pork sandwich from the covered area outside the store. A local BBQ restaurant had been talked into cooking lunches for people, paid for by the conference.

Gina was wolfing down her sandwich when one of the sheriffs, or maybe a deputy, sat down across from her. She couldn't really tell them apart. Hadn't given any of them a good look, she'd been so shocked about Delia's death. She still felt shocked.

"You're Gina Weatherby?"

"I am."

"I'm Sheriff Jansson. You're the one who found the body?" He pulled out a small black notebook and began writing.

She looked at him now. He was medium height and in good shape. She could see muscles under those long black sleeves. Probably in his sixties. Hard to tell. He shaved his head, as was the style for a lot of balding men these days. He had a nice smile and kind eyes with wrinkles around them.

"Delia. Yes."

"Tell me what happened," he said. "You don't work here, do you? No hoodie."

"No, I'm not an employee. I'm an artist, a botanical illustrator. I've been here all week, painting flowers for an upcoming show. Today, I ran out of clean water. So I went to the mist greenhouse, there's a faucet in there. Max, Delia's dog, was outside barking. Upset. He hardly ever barks. I let him in and he raced to the inside door. I let him in the mist section and was walking to the faucet when I saw her."

"What exactly did you see?"

"I saw Delia lying on her side between the plant benches. Not moving. Max licked her. I jiggled her and she rolled over on her back. That's when I saw the gash on her face."

"Nasty one that."

"She didn't respond. I thought she fell and hit her head, I didn't know she was dead. I stood up to run back to where I was working and called 911. Then I saw the bloody shovel under the plant bench. I didn't touch anything other than Delia."

"Where did you touch her?"

"Her shoulder, well, the shoulder of her hoodie."

"And then?"

"I ran back to the tropical greenhouse to get my phone. Called 911. Then called Melanie, my friend, who works here. I wanted someone here to know fast and didn't want to have to hunt anyone down. Melanie had been looking for Delia earlier. I told her to tell Renee, too. Then I came back here and waited till the medics arrived. Melanie came. Then Renee. Then when the medics told us Delia was dead, we left. Renee seemed to want to be alone. Then you or one of the other sheriffs or deputies came."

"It was me," he smiled.

"I'm not a very good witness, huh? Didn't even recognize you."

"It's the black uniform. We all look alike." He smiled.

She laughed at his joke and then realized that it felt awkward to laugh after Delia's death.

"Had you seen Delia earlier today, before you found her?"

"I saw her when I first got here this morning. I left home at 8, so it would've been 8:05, 8:10."

"You live close?"

"Just down on Alder Lane."

"Oh, there are some nice places there."

"There are some spectacular houses. Mine's nice, but smallish. I like it that way, less cleaning."

"Good for you. Life is too short to spend your time cleaning. So, do you know anyone who would have wanted to kill Delia?"

"Not a soul. I think her staff liked her, you'll have to ask them. She paid well, treated people fairly, it seemed. I know Karen, the nursery manager, moved out here from Edmonds just to take the job. This is a prestigious nursery. Delia was so well thought of in the plant world that the nursery was included in this conference even though it's a ways away from Seattle. The conference has drawn people from all over the world. You saw what it's been like today. It's been a zoo with so many customers. And I can't even think what the next three days are going to be like. Word about her death is bound to get out and the place will be flooded with people, unless you shut us down."

She should tell him about Delia and Renee's argument. It might mean something, but she doubted it.

Before she had a chance, Karen came into the tent and sat down next to the Sheriff, setting a soda on the table. Her normally energetic demeanor was gone. She brushed a hand through her short brown hair and let out a deep breath.

"You said to let you know if something's missing. I didn't have a lot of time, so I started with the mist greenhouse. At least three of Delia's rare plants are gone."

"Oh?" he said, raising his eyebrows.

"One is the Paeonia veitchii 'Variegata', maybe one of two in the world. Then the Hydrangea fragrans which was the only known plant in the world. Last, an unnamed plant, well it has a Vietnamese name, chua benh sau, it means deep healing. Delia brought it back from Vietnam. It's used there medicinally and is extremely rare as well."

"What does that mean?" asked Sheriff Jansson.

"It means that someone's gotten in our greenhouse and stolen three one of a kind plants. Plants no one else has. Plants that are rare and priceless."

"Could it have happened before today?" he asked.

"Delia would have noticed it. She was in there last night, watering and cleaning up. Checking on everything. I was here rearranging some things out front, so it looked good, and tidying up. If they was gone she would have said something."

Sheriff Jansson shifted in his chair.

"Could anyone actually sell them?"

"Good question," said Karen. "We have all of them under propagation. It's too soon to tell if any of them have taken. The Paeonia, there's two of those. The other one's owned by a Japanese collector. He may have gotten divisions off his plant by now. He traded Delia hers for another plant he wanted. They were both the same size and that was a few years ago. You have to divide them to propagate them and because of the variegation they're slow growing. We got two divisions off hers. It will be a decade or so before those are ready to divide. Provided they survive and thrive.There's not another plant that looks like it though. People will want it, mostly collectors. They pay the big bucks though."

Karen sipped her soda and said, "The Hydrangea, they grow easily from cuttings. This is the first truly fragrant one ever found. For Hydrangea breeders, getting their hands on the plant could be huge. They could tissue culture it and have it out in a year or two. It's going to bloom this year probably. They could let it cross with another hydrangea and hope the seedlings keep the fragrance, but they wouldn't know for a couple years probably. So, that plant's worth a ton of money to the nursery trade."

Karen sighed.

"The plant from Vietnam, we've been calling it chua for short, it's a wild card. It's rare. Gina and her guide in Vietnam are supposedly the only ones who know the location now. It's remote, high up some mountain in the jungle. The Vietnamese used it medicinally, long ago, but with the war and overuse most known patches of it got wiped out. The root was used to kill parasites, funguses, bacteria and possibly viruses. Delia's plan was to propagate it and sell plants to the drug companies. To replace antibiotics. To the drug companies it might be worth a lot, or nothing. It's all speculation until the drug trials are done. Without the plant though, and lots of them, the trials can't take place. That's why Delia wanted to make a lot of them to sell."

Gina sipped her cold water and marveled at what Karen had said.

"Would someone want any or all of these plants enough to murder for them?" asked the Sheriff. "I'm not a gardener. I don't understand this world."

Gina said, "I'm not a gardener either, but I've seen rare, and not so rare, plants sold for hundreds of dollars. There were two women this morning who almost came to blows over a fancy Solomon's seal that had buds on it, when there was a perfectly good one without buds sitting right next to it, one that would bloom next year. People who are plant collectors are all a bit crazy."

Karen smiled grimly and said, "What she said."

Sheriff Jansson shook his head. "I'm going to need to talk to all the staff. What time do you close today?"

"We're open late, because of the conference. We won't be closing till 6. Although the gardens close at 5, so some of us will be free earlier," said Karen.

"Don't let anyone go home till I've talked to them. I've got a few holes in my map of where everyone was this morning. And I need the phone number and address for David, the employee who's not here today."

"I'll get you that," Karen said. "You don't think David...?"

"I'm just collecting information, not ruling anyone out yet. Except perhaps Max. I don't think he's capable of lifting a shovel."

Gina's whole body clenched at that. That meant she was a suspect too. Then she took a deep breath. She'd done nothing wrong. She hadn't killed Delia. Even though she'd been nearby when it happened.

Who *had* killed Delia? And why?

She'd been so shocked at the murder to even ask. Shocked

that an acquaintance who she'd just seen and spoken to an hour or so before, was gone. Murdered.

"So you think Delia's death wasn't random?" asked Gina.

"It is possible, but no, I don't think so. I'm not sure if the theft of those plants is connected or separate though. I don't suppose you have a list of everyone who's come to the nursery today. Her murder happened just a couple hours before the nursery opened. Maybe the murderer came back under cover of the convention goers to see what effect they had."

So that's why he hadn't closed the nursery. Gina had wondered about why he hadn't.

Karen smiled and said, "I'll be right back."

Gina asked, "Do you know what time Delia was killed?"

"You saw her shortly after eight. They were searching for her at ten. We're guessing it's in that window. The coroner will be able to tell us more later."

"It's such an awful thing," Gina said.

"Yes. Yes, it is."

"I do need to tell you that I heard an argument between Delia and Renee."

"Oh?"

"They were standing outside the greenhouse where I was painting. And yelling at each other."

"When was this?"

"Sometime after I started painting. Maybe eight-thirty or nine."

"What were they arguing about?"

"Delia's infidelity with some guy. And that she wanted to let him become part of the business. He had a lot of money, she said."

"And they were yelling?"

"Yes. But I really can't see Renee being a murderer. She was mad, yes. And hurt. She refused to talk about it any more and stomped off."

"Then what happened?"

"I assume Delia left too. That was it."

"Well, thank you. That was very helpful. Did they argue often?"

"I don't work here, so I'm not around much. I've never seen them argue. I just assumed from what I'd seen that they were about as happy together as any couple."

"I wonder, could you remember enough of their fight to write it down?"

"I can try," she said.

Karen returned leading a roundish woman with shoulder-length blond hair. The woman was dressed in black pants and an artsy purple, fuchsia and black blouse.

"Pamela Hoffman, meet Sheriff Janssen. Pamela is the conference host and liaison for Ravenswood. She's volunteering at the conference and we're her post. She also does the newsletter and program. So she's been taking photos of every single person and their box of plants, while they wait to be checked out."

"Nice to meet you," said Pamela, in a southern accent enhanced by a bubbly personality that only those younger than thirty were able to pull off.

"And you've photographed everyone?" asked the Sheriff.

"Yes sir. Every single person who checked out. And I've been popping out here and getting photos of people eating lunch, too." She held up her cell phone. "I also put together the badges for the conference and so I made it my business to learn everyone's names and faces."

"But if people didn't buy anything, you didn't photograph them," said the Sheriff.

"No, but the shop has a great view of the parking lot. I remember who carpooled together. And there were only three, no four people, who didn't buy anything at all. Three Australians and one of the Japanese. It was probably too much work to get the plants through customs. They'll mail order instead if they want plants. All the Americans bought at least one plant. So did the English. There are so many amazing plants here. I've got a whole carload picked out."

"So, it's possible for the international convention goers to bring plants back to their countries?" the Sheriff asked Karen.

"It varies by country," said Karen. "We provide a phytosanitary certificate for our plants. That gets them through in a lot of places. Some countries are more restrictive and the plants have to go through quarantine. It gets very complicated. Sometimes the plants need to be free of soil, for quite a while depending on the staffing at customs. That doesn't make plants very happy."

"I would imagine not," said Sheriff Jansson. "The plants that are missing, could they survive that?"

"They already have," said Karen. "That's how Delia brought them into the country. And all of them were in prime condition when I last saw them. The process wouldn't take such a toll on them."

Sheriff Jansson asked Pamela, "Can you get me a list of the conference attendees and send me all the photos you've taken here?" He handed her a card from his shirt pocket.

"Sure, I'd be happy too. I'll have to wait till I get home though. My phone battery's dying and the attendee list is on my computer."

"That'll be fine. Will you be here tomorrow too?"

"Yes, I'm here every day of the conference. I love this nursery!"

"Good, I might need help with identifying people in the photos."

"So, is it true that Delia was murdered? The conference people have been looking for her all day," said Pamela

"I can't comment on what's happened at this time," he said.

Pamela looked as if someone slapped her.

Gina sipped her water. What if the murderer had simply

wandered through the property? She was really hoping it wasn't anyone she knew, however unlikely that might be.

Another crowd of people had finished the garden tour and were shopping or standing in line for lunch.

Gina said, "Well, I'd better get back to helping out and open up a table." She needed to be busy and not be pondering who killed Delia.

Karen said, "Thanks so much, Gina. I'll make sure you get put on the payroll. We really needed you today. What are you doing the next three days?"

"Helping out?" Gina asked.

"Awesome," said Karen.

"Maybe by tomorrow I'll have figured out where all the plants are at."

They all got up from the table and Gina tossed her garbage.

The Sheriff said, "I'll need to talk to you again, too. Before you go back and help, could you go somewhere quiet and write down that conversation you overheard?"

She didn't want to even think of it anymore, but if it would help find Delia's killer, then she would. She sure hoped it wasn't Renee.

"I'll go back to the greenhouse. I have a notepad in my bag."

"Good."

Gina went back to the tropical greenhouse, pulled her notebook and pen out. She tore a page out of the back and wrote down everything she could remember, which was quite a lot. Then stuck the page into her jeans pocket to give to the Sheriff.

She felt like a tattletale. But then again, if Renee had murdered Delia, she would get what she deserved. Infidelity, awful though it was, wasn't enough of an excuse to take someone's life.

She looked for the Sheriff, but couldn't find him. She'd better go help out, the nursery was packed.

Gina went back to the information center near the greenhouses.

When was she going to get her painting finished? It had better be before that Hibiscus ran out of blossoms. Maybe she should come in earlier tomorrow, get some time to paint before the nursery opened?

Gina shuddered. She sure didn't feel comfortable being alone at the nursery. Not after today.

A man came up and broke into her thoughts.

"Hello, can you tell me where to find your Podophyllums?" he asked in a delightful English accent.

"Which one are you looking for?"

"All of them."

"Well, the map says there are some in greenhouse 3, on the west side. There are others in greenhouse 6, east side and the south end, and in greenhouse 7, also east side, at the south end. The directions are marked on the greenhouse walls."

"Why does Delia split them all up like that?" he asked.

"I'm guessing that if they lose their tags, she wants the staff to have a chance of identifying them by keeping the different varieties separate."

"Well, that makes sense, thank you." He was off, cardboard box in hand.

The next few hours went by in a blur. Gina kept looking for the Sheriff, but the one time he went by, he was in hurry and she couldn't catch him. It felt like the record of Delia and Renee's argument was burning a hole in her pocket. It kept her mind tugging at the question of who murdered Delia, just like a terrier.

Just as soon as she'd have an idea some customer would show up and she'd get dragged away from her thoughts by a customer. Going back and forth was exhausting. She'd rarely seen the nursery this busy, but then she didn't hang out here that much.

When the gardens closed at five, Karen, Melanie and Brianna were freed up to work in the nursery. Gina took a break. She went into the tropical greenhouse and began cleaning up her brushes and putting her paint away.

Sheriff Jansson came in.

"Oh, there you are. I have some more questions," he took out his notebook and pen.

"Here's what I can remember of the argument," she said, pulling the paper out of her pocket, unfolding it and giving it to him. That gave her a small sense of relief.

"Thank you," he said, looking it over.

"I thought I'd pack up. The light will be gone shortly and I'm not getting any more painting done today." She didn't know how she'd get all the paintings done in time for the show. She'd just have to paint some at night. From photographs.

"That's beautiful," he said, looking at her painting.

"Thank you. It's not done. I'm going to have to come in early tomorrow. Before the nursery opens. Although I don't feel very safe." She folded the cover of the pad over the painting and slid it into a pocket of the bag.

"The deputies will still be here. I might even be here."

"That would help a lot," she said. "I know Karen will be here. There's watering to do. But she'll be at the far end of the nursery probably." Gina put her empty water bottle and paint cup into the bag.

"So, if you had to guess who killed Delia, what would your guess be? Who would benefit from Delia's death?"

"I have no idea. I can't see anyone who works here doing it. I don't know them all well, though. Melanie's my closest friend. I know she didn't do it. She has nothing to gain and she's just doesn't have any reason to hurt anyone. She's already retired and just working for a bit of extra money to support her plant habit. And I know I didn't do it. I can't believe Karen could do it. I know she wants to open her own nursery some day, which would mean leaving here. But the island has room for two nurseries. So many people drive up here from Seattle and down from Bellingham.

Visiting two nurseries would just be cake and frosting. They'd be different. Karen loves different plants than Delia. Please don't write what I say down. It's all just me blathering on."

"This is for my own personal use. Most likely no one else will see it, but you might say something important that solves the case. Details are important. Tell me about the others," he said.

"Stacy, the cashier, I don't know much about her. Or Tyler or David. They're all kids. Barely twenty. Well, Tyler probably isn't even that. Brianna mostly does mail order, I've talked with her a bit. She's newly married. And pregnant. I don't think she's really committed to working here. When she has her baby, she'll already have been laid off for the season."

"Laid off? Why?"

"Working in nurseries is almost always seasonal work. People get hired for the busy season, work like crazy, sometimes more than full time, then when the season ends in late summer or fall, nurseries lay everyone off that they can. There's no money coming in. People stop buying plants. This nursery has a bit more solid year-round income, Melanie says. It attracts the hard core gardeners and mail order often happens before spring sets in. And in this region people garden all year round, the climate's mild enough. But even so Delia lays off everyone who isn't absolutely essential."

"So there might be hard feelings about that."

"She tells everyone she hires that they'll be laid off at the end of the summer. And it's still early, some of them have only been working for a month now. Also, Tyler, Stacy and the others, I don't know if they know plants well enough to understand how rare and priceless those missing plants are. If an employee wanted to steal plants, there are probably better times to do it than when there's a major event going on here."

"But the event would provide a lot of distraction," said the Sheriff.

"True, but Delia was going plant hunting next week. She

would have been gone for two weeks. That would have been a better time to steal her plants. And the nursery's only open four days a week, even though staff's here seven. Stealing plants on one of those closed days when Delia's gone and things are more relaxed would be a lot smarter. Most of the staff will be out working in the gardens, not watching the parking lot for customers."

"You've given this a lot of thought."

"When I'm here painting, my brain rambles on in all sorts of directions. And often I paint outside, near the store because that's where they put the most glorious displays. Sometimes customers arrive on the closed days and I have to turn them away. It's come to my attention how easy it would be to walk off with things. But I'm not a gardener. I just like painting plants, so I'm safe. I am so done with care-taking!"

He laughed.

"What about Renee? Delia's partner."

"Well, I don't know much about their relationship. They seemed to get along just fine. They've been together for fifteen years. Ten years ago they opened the nursery. I like Renee, she does have a temper though. I always knew Delia had a wandering eye, but I thought it was just her eyes. There were rumors about a fling Delia had on a plant collecting trip a few years back. With some Englishman. Don't know if there's any truth to it."

"Does this Englishman have a name?"

"Mark Morris. Big name plantsman. He's written a lot of books. Delia was always quoting him, 'Mark says this plant is just the best' or 'Mark says that plant's a dud'. She was always going on about him. But like I said, I don't know if there was anything beyond professional respect."

"What about the drug companies? Had Delia contacted any of them?"

"I don't know. You should ask Karen or Renee about that."

"So, no guesses about a murderer?"

"Out of everybody we talked about? None of them seem likely. Renee would have the best reason to kill her, if Delia had been sleeping around. But she wouldn't have any reason to steal the plants. It must be someone who doesn't work here."

"Unless the plants and the murder aren't related."

"In that case, I'm still going with my theory of the random, crazy person hiking through the woods."

"That makes you feel safer?"

"No, but it's better than thinking the people you see on a regular basis are murderers."

"Well, I believe we're all capable of killing someone if the circumstances are right."

"I just don't."

"C'mon. Do you have children?"

"Yes. All grown up and living on their own now."

"But, when they were little, if someone attacked you and you couldn't run, get your kids to safety: wouldn't you have stayed to defend them?"

"Yes."

"And you might have been trying to immobilize an attacker, but if you hit them hard enough or just at the right angle with a broom handle, it might have killed them. When I was still a young man, I and many of my friends were called off to war. Whether or not it was a 'good cause', it was killing someone. We're all capable, given the right circumstances."

"Accidentally killing someone while defending yourself, or children, is different than hunting someone down and murdering them."

"I'd like to believe that. It's all the same to the person who died. But there we meander over into the realm of philosophy. Some people wouldn't agree. I have to work under what the law says. I make the arrests and let the courts decide."

"I still think there's a difference between self-defense and murder."

"The end result is a dead human body. And that's a shame."

A loud gong rang, echoing over all the nursery.

"Closing," said Gina. She folded her easel and stowed it in the bag. She zipped up the pocket and picked it up along with her raincoat.

"Well, thank you for the enlightening conversation," Sheriff Jansson said.

"You're welcome. I hope it helps, but like I said, I don't know much."

"Seems to me like you know a lot."

She laughed. "I'm full of opinions about everything under the sun."

He walked her out of the greenhouse and to the front of the nursery.

Karen was there, waiting. She held out a hoodie for Gina.

"It's a large, that's all I could find. We need to reorder. I hope it's not too big."

"Thanks," said Gina. "It will be fine. That way I can wear a sweater under it if I need to."

"I'll have paperwork for you tomorrow, a W-2 and stuff."

"What time will you get here?"

"About seven."

"Good, I'd like to come early and get that Hibiscus painted before it goes out of bloom and I lose my chance."

"I'm sorry you didn't get to finish it today. Thank you so much for stepping in and helping."

"You're welcome. See you tomorrow morning. Bye everyone."

"I'd like to talk to you about the nursery's security system," the Sheriff said to Karen.

Gina nearly burst out laughing.

Karen did.

"We have no security system."

Gina walked down the path towards the parking lot. Melanie stood by her pickup, waiting for Gina.

She could still hear as Sheriff Jansson asked, "What do you do with cash at the end of the day?"

"Delia drove it to the bank. There usually wasn't much. Most of our business is checks or plastic."

"There's no alarms or anything?" he asked.

"We don't even have a gate for the parking lot. There are motion detector lights, out near the greenhouses. Those are mostly for emergencies. In the winter someone has to go knock snow off the greenhouses every few hours so they don't collapse. It often snows at night here and Delia got tired of doing it by flashlight. So she saved that delight for when the power goes out."

Gina walked out of earshot of their conversation.

Melanie said, "I'm starving and all I've got at home is some truly awful soup I made. Want to go out for dinner? I can't possibly relax, not after today."

Gina was really tired. She'd only planned to paint for a few hours and then go home and cook dinner.

"Me neither. I'm so keyed up. I'd love to go out, but I've got to go home first. Feed the monsters and get out of these filthy clothes. Plus, rubber boots," she said, holding out a foot.

"I stayed pretty clean, just leading people around the gardens. I'll follow you and we can drive in my pickup."

"Deal," said Gina.

She put her bag in the car and extracted her cell phone from the back pocket of her jeans before getting into the car. She slipped it in her purse and drove home.

Melanie pulled up in front of the house and followed her inside.

Alice and Albert meowed at her, making circles around her legs.

"Yes, I know. It's an hour past your dinner and you're going to starve," Gina said to them, putting down her bag, purse, coat and hat. She opened a large can of food and plopped it into two bowls which she set on the floor.

Each cat dove for a bowl and eagerly ate.

"Wow, I didn't think cats did that."

"These two eat like dogs. I think it's a competition thing."

"Well, they're so huge."

"They are big, but not as big as the hair. You should see them when they're wet, half the size."

Gina washed her hands, dirty from handling plants all day. Then she changed into a clean t-shirt, jeans, socks and slip-on shoes. Ran a brush through her short hair and checked to make sure her face was clean.

She pulled a fleece jacket out of the coat closet and slipped it on. Then picked up her purse and said, "Where do you want to go?"

"I don't know," said Melanie. "Mexican, pizza, fish?"

"I could go for some fish and chips."

"And beer?"

"I could definitely use a beer after today."

"Me too. The Marina it is."

The Marina was a kitchy seafood place frequented by tourists. But the food was wonderful and the beer selection unparalleled.

It was a busy Friday night, but the hostess recognized them and put them near a window, away from most of the crowds. The bar was especially noisy. The smells coming from the kitchen were amazing. Garlic, butter and fish. Gina's stomach growled in anticipation.

The restaurant held about fifty tables with ten more in the bar. The entire place was made of old wood and stone to create a subdued color scheme of warm browns and grays brightened with crimson accents. The tables were square and circular, ancient and possibly antiques. The chairs mismatched and wood as well. There were crimson linen napkins and sparkling silver, but otherwise the tables sat bare, encouraging customers to take up the space. No hokey candles or salt and pepper shakers, although every single window was decorated with shells, buoys and driftwood, which looked tacky to Gina. Holes drilled in them, the beach debris was strung with tarred twine and draped in a zig-zag across the glass.

The food was served as the cook, Mitch, wanted it to be served. Once Gina had seen a man demand salt and Mitch had come out of the kitchen and told him that he'd already salted it. If he didn't like it, he could leave and not pay without eating. Mitch was a gentle, but imposing 6'3", burly man. The startled customer had reconsidered.

The sky had grown dark outside on the ride over. The lights across Puget Sound shimmered on the rough water. Wind was picking up.

"They're forecasting a storm for tonight or tomorrow," said Melanie.

"Big one?"

"Maybe. Mostly 30-40 mph winds. A few gusts of 60."

"That's not good for the nursery, is it?" Gina's mind was on what tomorrow would bring. Saturday was supposed to be the busiest conference day at the nursery. And there was sure to be a lot of turmoil and drama once word got out of Delia's death. She really didn't want to be there, but she'd agreed to help out again.

"Nope, but we've got a generator for the cash register. And the internet's satellite, so we might still be able to ring up credit cards. If not, we'll be doing things the old fashioned way. But nearly all our customers are honest, so we'll just use one of those old style card machines and not verify if the card's good."

"What about flinging branches and stuff?"

"We hope it doesn't happen. Delia had arborists come out twice a year to look for problems. They removed anything injured, dying or dead they find. She didn't want things to fall on the garden and take out or maim a priceless plant. But even the arborists say they can't see everything."

Their server came to the table. Misty.

"Well good evening ladies, do you know what you want yet?"

"I'll have fish and chips and the spring rye ale with coriander," said Gina.

"And I'll have fish & chips. And an IPA, let's see. Oh this one, the Boundary Bay."

"Okay, I'll bring the beer right away."

Misty disappeared in the dimness of the restaurant, weaving between tables and partitions.

"Wow, they must be busy, she's not talking," said Melanie.

Gina smiled. Misty was an incredible gossip. She knew everything about everyone in this town and the surrounding ones.

She returned with their beer and set them down.

"Hey, you work at Ravenswood don't you, Melanie?"

"I do."

"So, what happened?"

"What do you mean?"

"Who died?"

"Someone died?" asked Melanie, looking shocked as if she'd just heard it for the first time.

"There were a group of plant people in this evening. They all wore badges from some conference. They had just come from the nursery. I got to chatting with them and they said someone on the staff had died. They were thinking it was Delia, because no one had seen her."

"I had no idea," said Melanie. "I didn't work today. I was over in Arlington, visiting my daughter. She has a new baby. Just got back and picked up Gina. I couldn't face cooking."

Gina kept a straight face. Melanie did have a daughter in Arlington and she did have a new baby, a couple of months ago.

"Well, then you can't tell me anything," said Misty, her mouth pouting with disappointment.

"No, sorry."

"David was in here earlier tonight, too. With his girlfriend, looking all romancey. He couldn't tell me anything either."

"David was here," asked Melanie.

"Yeah. Those two look so happy together. Such a cute couple."

Misty said, "Well, gotta get back to work."

After she left, Melanie said, "That jerk. Didn't come to work today because of stomach flu, but was out with his girlfriend tonight. And he knew it was going to be a busy day."

"What if he did come to work?" asked Gina, quietly.

"What do you mean?" asked Melanie.

"What if he came to work, killed Delia and left?"

"Why would he kill Delia?"

"Why would anyone?" asked Gina. She told Melanie about the argument she'd overheard.

"Wow, and I thought everything was fine between them. But I still don't think Renee could do such a thing."

"Me neither."

"I think it was about the stolen plants," said Melanie.

"Did he know what they were worth?"

"We all did. He might not know how to sell them though. But he could have been working with someone who did."

"Who?" asked Gina.

They stopped talking as Misty set their beer on the table. She just smiled and left quickly, not saying anything. It must be busy tonight.

Gina sipped her rye ale and looked at Melanie questioningly.

"Mark Morris was there today. Maybe he decided the plants would be worth killing for."

"Was he there? I don't know what he looks like. He'd know how to sell them, wouldn't he?"

"Yes. David could be working with him. Or one of the drug companies. I know Delia had contacted them. They could get the plant for free that way. Not have to pay her exorbitant prices."

"But why would they take all three? Why not just take the one from Vietnam?"

"To confuse things. Otherwise, we'd know it was one of the drug companies."

"My mind just won't let go of this problem. I've been thinking about it all day. Trying to figure out who would do such a thing."

"Yeah, me too. It was really hard to lead people around the garden. There are plants out there that are going to bloom this year for the first time and Delia won't be there to see them." Melanie began to tear up and dabbed at her eyes with the linen napkin. Then she drank some beer.

"Do you think Renee will close the nursery?" asked Gina. "Or if the Sheriff will?"

"I don't know. I was going to order something for her and take it over tonight. I don't think she'll be cooking. Wanna come with?"

"Would I be in the way?"

"I think you might lighten things up a bit. I checked on her earlier in the day. Asked if there was anyone I could call, but she said no. When she came out, years ago, her family cut ties with her. So she made a new one. But it was all connected with Delia and plants. So actually, no. I don't think she'll close the nursery."

"It would be a shame if that happened. The garden is so incredible. Not another one like it anywhere."

"That's true, but I'm not looking forward to the next several days. We should talk to Renee tonight about spreading the word of Delia's death. People need to know," said Melanie

"Well, you have a better idea of what that means to the plant community than I do."

"It's important. Her life was important. She changed so much, brought so many species into cultivation. The garden at Ravenswood has transformed the way we garden in this region, what constitutes a beautiful garden."

"I'll go with you to see Renee tonight."

"Good. I think we all need to stick together. Everyone's a suspect," said Melanie.

"Oh, right. Except Max."

Melanie looked puzzled.

"That's what the Sheriff said. Only Max has been excluded from the list. He can't swing a shovel."

"Well, that's something at least," said Melanie, smiling slightly. "The only people I'm sure about are you and me. I know neither one of us did it."

Misty came back with their food.

"Did what?" she asked.

"Signed me up for a May Day show at Mason Gallery. I don't know how I'm going to get my paintings finished in time."

"Oh, good for you," said Misty. "When is it?"

"May Day. May first."

"Oh, duh. Well, enjoy your food, ladies."

"Thanks Misty," said Gina.

"We've really got to watch what we say," said Melanie.

Gina nodded, her mouth full of hot, succulent halibut and tartar sauce. Mitch made the best food. She closed her eyes in delight.

After dinner, they drove back to the nursery and parked in Renee's driveway. All the lights in the log cabin were on. They knocked and the door opened, Max lunging out to welcome them, his tongue flapping.

"Come in. I knew I could answer the door," Renee said, "because Max was standing at the door after you knocked, jumping up and down and wagging his tail. He recognized you through the door."

"Hi," said Melanie.

"We brought you some dinner," said Gina. "We know you love Mitch's cooking as much as we do."

"You went to the Marina? I tell ya, if I wasn't gay, I'd marry that man. Even if he's old enough to be my father. Wow, that's twisted."

"You're entitled to your twisted," said Melanie.

Gina had never been inside the house. It was warm and welcoming. She knew it had three bedrooms, two of which were used as individual offices. The inside had been decorated with wall hangings and paintings in tones of yellow ochre, deep red and black. Renee had a graphic design background and the interior of the house showed that. Everything looked perfect. Leather furniture in deep red and black fit the log cabin look, but was also perfectly modern. The wood and brass tables accented everything just so. Bookshelves filled with plant and garden books fit right in. The place gave off a cozy feeling, but also one of control and perfection.

The only thing that didn't fit were the cluttered kitchen table and counters. Covered with half-filled mugs of coffee and tea. A few dirty dishes. And piles upon piles of papers.

And Renee, looking disheveled and red-eyed.

"How are you doing?" asked Melanie.

"I'm alive. That's about all that can be said for me." Renee stood numbly in the middle of the kitchen. "One minute I'm weeping my eyes out, the next minute I want to kill her myself."

"Here, sit down," said Melanie, clearing away some of the mugs and creating a place at the table.

Gina took a plate out of the open cupboard and slid the fish and chips on it. She set it in front of Renee, along with a paper napkin.

"Can I get you something to drink?" she asked Renee.

Renee waved at the multiple cups and said, "I've been making myself coffee and tea all day long and forgetting to drink them."

"Water it is," said Gina. She poured a glass from the tap and set it near the plate.

"Now eat. Or we'll send Mitch after you," said Melanie, sitting down.

Gina sat at the table too.

Renee ate all of the fish and most of the fries.

"I don't think I've eaten since breakfast," she said. "It's been an awful day."

"What can we do to help?" asked Gina.

"You've already helped so much. Karen told me how you stepped in today and helped people find plants. Delia would have had something clever to say to you."

Renee began to cry and grabbed a tissue from the box on the table.

"Delia was an amazing woman. So are you," said Gina.

"Yes, she was. I was so blessed to have her in my life and I'm so angry and depressed that she's gone. I feel all mixed up. I know she was having an affair. That didn't mean I stopped loving her. Or that she stopped loving me, I think. It was just a fling. Him, I'd like to kill."

They said nothing.

"I shouldn't say things like that," Renee said. "I'm such a mess right now."

"You're allowed to be a mess," said Gina. "It's what we do when those we love go away. We fall apart. I wouldn't say things like that in front of the sheriff, though."

Renee looked at her. "You've met him then. He's wicked smart. Hides it all behind that easy going, *I'm your best friend you can tell me anything* act, though."

"I noticed that," said Melanie.

"I'm not sure it's an act. I think that's who he is," said Gina.

"You think he genuinely likes people?" asked Renee.

"I like to think the best of people. That he really does like people, but is determined to do his job and follow the law. At least that's the impression I got," said Gina.

"Gina, that's why I love hanging out with you. You're such an optimist," said Melanie.

"When did you last see Delia?" asked Gina. "What was she doing?"

Would Renee tell them about the fight? And who the investor

might be? Was he the same one Delia had a fling with? Was it Mark Morris or someone else?

"Just normal stuff. A couple of the water lines in the mist tent have been clogged all week. So on Thursday afternoon David fixed them. At least that's what he was supposed to do. We left on Thursday afternoon to go out to dinner with friends in town for the conference, in Seattle. Friday morning Delia had her coffee and a couple of sausages. Then she was off to make sure everything was good in the nursery. She left here about seven. To check the mist tent and make sure David fixed it and all the cuttings were getting misted. She also went to check that the displays were still upright, after the windstorm, and that they looked good. If there was time, she was going to take a quick walk through the gardens."

"The gardens and displays were perfect," said Melanie.

They stayed for another half hour, but Gina learned nothing else about Delia's death. It was getting late and they all had to be up early in the morning.

"I'm going to be in the nursery tomorrow," said Renee.

"You don't have to, you know," said Melanie.

"I do, though. It's important. I've got to keep things going. Delia would have wanted that. I've got to be the face of the nursery now."

"In the long run," Gina said, "it's not about what Delia would have wanted. It's about what you want. You have to do that."

"I know. That might change with time. But right now, I want to keep the nursery going. Make it grow. That's always been my part of the nursery. We just need to find another innovator, because without innovation, all that Delia did will die and I don't want that."

The drive home was quiet. Both of them talked out.

"You still going in early tomorrow?" Melanie asked.

"I don't want to. Not after today, but those paintings aren't going to paint themselves."

"Well, I'll see you when I get there. If Renee is going to be out there, we'll let her handle the front end and plants. You'd be great in the garden, doing plant tours. We have a lot of garden design people. You could point out things that Karen or I might not notice."

"I could do that," said Gina. "But I don't know the plants."

"Everything's tagged and there are stepping stones in all the beds. You are allowed to go in and check, not customers though. And even if you don't know the name of a plant, half of your group will."

"I'm willing to try. I can't believe Renee's going to be worth anything as far as helping customers. I was a mess for months after Ewan died."

Gina went inside and fell into bed fairly quickly. Surrounded by two piles of purring fur. She tossed and turned, running scenarios through her head.

Who could have murdered Delia?

DAY 2 - SATURDAY

Gina woke in the morning to a wet nose rubbing against her own. She groaned and rolled over, then glanced at the clock. The alarm was going off in five minutes.

"Brat," she said to Alice.

Alice gave her the starving meow and Albert joined in.

"All right. I'm up." Her body ached from yesterday. Standing all day and moving plants around.

She fed the cats and went into the bathroom to splash cold water on her face. This morning was going to take a lot of coffee. She normally drank tea, then again she normally slept well.

Last night she kept waking up. Her mind searching for answers. Who murdered Delia? Holding onto that question, unable to let it go unanswered. Of course the puzzle hadn't been solved overnight.

She hoped the Sheriff would be there today. She had some thoughts for him. Although they were probably things he'd already considered.

While dressing, Gina made a pot of coffee. She poured some into a cup to drink now and the rest into a thermos for later. Then added cream to each. She sipped the coffee and rolled the rich liquid around in her mouth. Lovely.

Gina toasted an English muffin and spread it with almond butter. She interspersed bites with those of a banana in an attempt to eat a balanced breakfast. For lunch there would be more of that yummy pulled pork.

She finished eating and rinsed the dishes, putting them in the dishwasher.

Alice was already asleep again. Alfred sat on one of the kitchen chairs giving her the look.

"Yes, I'm leaving again. Come here you big lug." She picked him up and he began to purr, a loud rumbling purr that she could feel even through all his fur and her t-shirt. She buried her face in his soft fur.

"Love ya buddy, but I gotta get going. I'll be home in time to feed you dinner." She set him down on the back of the couch. A blue jay landed on the deck railing and began squawking raucously. That got his attention.

Gina pulled the Ravenswood hoodie on and stuffed her rain coat and hat into her painting bag. Just in case. She opted for running shoes today. Wet or not, they'd be more comfortable for standing the whole day.

She pulled up at the nursery at 7:30. The Sheriff's and Deputy's cars were already there. That made her feel safer, although Gina didn't think she'd be a target. The murderer had most likely been looking for Delia, or the plants.

Gina decided to leave her rain gear in the car. She slid her phone into a zip pocket of the hoodie. Not that she was expecting a call, but she never wore a watch anymore.

The sun came out from behind the clouds, promising a bit of warmth for the day. The smells of moisture, soil and green plants came to her nose as she walked through the nursery. It was a kind of freshness, the smell of living things.

She heard voices. The Sheriff and Deputy were on the far side of the mist greenhouse. She saw their flashlight beams. It was dark over there at this time of morning, beneath the deep shade of the cedars. Had the murderer been hiding there, waiting for Delia? Or had they escaped that way?

Gina went into the tropical greenhouse. The humidity struck her once again. The smell of damp soil was stronger here, nearly masked by the jasmine. That was it, jasmine, not Gardenia. Sweet and spicy scented. It almost made her feel comfortable.

She set up her easel and painting supplies. Today, she'd brought a larger water bottle, not sure if she'd be able to go into the mist greenhouse and get water there. It still had crime scene tape on it. And she didn't want to go all the way back to the store area, where all the hoses would be coiled up.

By the time other people arrived, she'd finished off the thermos of coffee and the Hibiscus painting. She'd started another painting of a rather exotic orchid in colors of cream, maroon and black. Not a frilly, blowsy flower like the Hibiscus, but a dramatic blossom for people whose homes called for that kind of art.

Melanie popped her head in the door and Gina jumped.

"Sorry to scare you. I guess we're all a bit jumpy. You getting your painting done?"

"Yes. The Hibiscus was the worry. Those flowers only last a day or so."

"Good. Do you need a garden map when you give tours?"

"Yeah, I should have one."

"I'll get you one. Come to the store at about a quarter to nine. I'm sure customers will be here early, but tours start at nine."

"So, we're open today?"

"Sheriff says yes. Just keep people out of the roped off area."

"Okay, I'll be ready."

Gina glanced at her phone. Twenty minutes. The wash she'd done would take that long to dry. She might as well pack up and put everything in her car. Then she could do the detail work tomorrow morning.

She cleaned up the brushes and put them away. Left the painting pad open so it would dry. She'd torn off the page with the Hibiscus painting, but it was still wet. They'd dry in the car. She stuck the easel in her bag. Picked up the bag and carried the two paintings, each held out flat on an arm, to her car. The Sheriff stood near the store, talking to Karen.

"Good morning," he said.

"Good morning," she waved a hand slightly, so as not to drop the painting.

"You're not leaving?" he asked.

"No, just putting these in the car."

"Oh, let me see," said Karen.

"This one's done. Mostly. I might still do some ink work on it," said Gina, handing her the hibiscus painting. "The other one's just started, nothing to see yet."

"This is gorgeous. I'm going to need to go see that show," said Karen.

"What show?" asked the Sheriff, sipping a cup of coffee. She recognized the purple paper cup from one of the espresso stands in town.

"The Mason Gallery is having a May Day Show and wanted paintings of flowers," said Gina.

"And the paintings will be for sale?" he asked.

"Yes."

"I might have to pick one of these up," he said. "The apartment could use a little help."

"They'll be there. I've got five more to paint. And frame. Well, I better get these put away, so I can get to work," said Gina.

Cars were pouring into the parking lot. By the time the nursery opened, there were enough people for three groups to begin touring the gardens. The bulk of people wanted to shop first and get the better choice of plants. Of course, the first pick had been yesterday, but there were still plenty of exotic plants. And everyone had different gardening styles and bought different plants.

Melanie handed Gina the tour map and showed her the route she should take so there wouldn't be too many traffic jams between the three groups.

Renee came out of the store. She'd made an effort to look good, although her eyes were still red. She wore jeans and a Ravenswood hoodie, but had put her hair up, wore makeup and earrings.

She said to the staff, "I'm going to make an announcement to the customers here about Delia's death. I've also put a notice up on the side of the store. Beyond those, none of us can say anything else. Her death is still being investigated by the Raven Island Sheriff's Department. We'll have the conference send out another announcement that says the same thing."

Gina noticed a gangly young man, wearing a Ravenswood hoody, standing behind Karen. He looked ill at ease. Must be David. David who called in sick yesterday, but obviously hadn't been. He had sandy brown hair and pale skin. She didn't like him, but who knew if he was a murderer? She needed to tell the Sheriff about that.

Sheriff Jansson stood behind the employees taking everything in.

She motioned to him and they walked a ways off from the others.

"I have something to tell you," she said.

"I'm listening."

"David wasn't too sick to take his girlfriend out for dinner last night. Melanie and I went out and our waitress said she'd seen them earlier in the night."

"Where?"

"The Marina. Just thought you should know."

"Thank you," he said. "Please let me know if you find anything else out."

"I will," she said.

Renee walked over to the group of customers who were patiently waiting to be let into the nursery.

"Good morning. We're all pleased to see you on this glorious spring morning. Some of you may have heard that we had a death in our family yesterday. I'm making it public today. Delia Swanson, the co-owner and co-founder of Ravenswood Nursery was found dead yesterday morning. We are all shocked and saddened by the loss of a great plant hunter, innovator and irreplaceable friend. But we also realize this might be your first, only, or last, visit to our nursery. So we'll be doing the best we can to make your visit perfect. Please be patient with us. And enjoy. The gardens are in their spring glory, the greenhouses are stuffed with plants looking for good homes. In an hour or so, a local company, the BBQ Brothers, will be firing up the food. We have lots of staff on hand to help you find what you're looking for. Thanks for coming! Those of you who want to tour the gardens first, please stay in this courtyard. The rest of you, the nursery is open!"

People rushed towards the greenhouses, many with paper lists in hand, others had notes on their phones. Still others moved into the courtyard where Renee divided them into three groups.

Gina gathered her group around her and said, "We're going to start with the more natural sections of the garden and move to the more cultivated last. First off are the wild woodland and the boggy area. I have to warn you, I'm not a gardener, I'm an artist. I look at gardens in terms of their balance, the textures, colors and design. I do have a plant key for the gardens here, but it's the same one you have. If you have specific questions about how to care for a plant, Karen is the nursery manager and she'll be spending her time helping people find plants, and would be happy to answer your questions."

Gina led the twenty people off down the gravel path through the tall cedar, big leaf maple and hemlock forest. The trees were giants, one person couldn't wrap both arms around any of the trees and still feel their fingers touch. They were underplanted with native evergreen sword ferns, soft and graceful maidenhair ferns and rubbery looking deer ferns. There were many species of Mahonia with their sharp, holly-like leaves. Their heights ranged from ground cover to twelve feet tall. Some of them still had yellow blooms which the hummingbirds visited. Others had dropped the blossoms and berries were forming. Flowering currants interspersed the Mahonia, with drooping blooms of white, pale pink or bright pink. Some of the latter also had chartreuse leaves which brightened up the dark areas beneath the tall trees.

"Are any of these plants medicinal?" asked a tall, thin man with very pale skin and glasses. This was the third time he'd asked if something was medicinal, which drew her attention to him.

"I don't know. Many are edible. One of the Mahonia species is called Oregon grape. The berries are sometimes made into jams and syrups, with a lot of sugar, because they're mouth-puckering tart. Hemlock needles, new spring green ones, can be nibbled on. I know some fern fronds are edible, as are some of the young maple leaves of some species, but as far as I know none of these plants are used medicinally. Except our native Digitalis," she said.

Gina touched a flowering stalk of a perennial. "Commonly called foxglove, heart medicine has been made from this plant. It's just budding up and won't open for a month or so. Pink, white or cerise flowers with spots inside. I'll let you know if we come across something that is used medicinally."

The man nodded. His conference badge said Jonathon Ashley.

She continued on through the woodland with its ephemeral beauties to the swamp where the skunk cabbage, yellow and white, were in full bloom. The most alien appearing flowers, they looked plastic. A fingerlike spadix, protected by the hoodlike spathe. Green leaves, the same size as the spathe, would continue growing throughout the season until they were three to four feet long and a foot or two wide.

"Water floods in here all winter long from our rains. The entire property drains to this site. In the summer it dries out enough that we need to water occasionally. I love the gaudiness of the yellow and white flowers. Behind them are red, yellow and orange, twig dogwood shrubs. We cut them to the ground every spring to keep the stems brightly colored. These are mostly variegated, with either yellow or white, so they're lovely to look at in the summer too."

On the sunny section of the bog, she pointed out the patch of carnivorous plants.

"These are Sarracenia species, pitcher plants. And those are Darlingtonia californica, cobra lilies, they both like wet feet, but the Darlingtonia want to be planted a bit higher. They do well in this part of the world and have the most dramatic flowers."

She touched one of the pitcher plant flowers, on a long, sticklike stem with a drooping flowerhead of single crimson-purple petal surrounding a greenish open ball like center. The plants looked exotic and alien, the flowers even more so.

"How many species of pitcher plant are here?" asked a middle-aged woman with a hot pink hoodie.

"Ten different types of pitcher plants and just the one cobra lily. We have more than these for sale, some are newer cultivars. This bed's been here for ten years. I know there's a new cobra lily that gets much larger than the species. We just haven't gotten it in the ground out here."

"And they eat bugs?"

"Yes, the sap inside the tubular leaves is attractive to insects.

They crawl in and can't get back out. Sometimes spiders make their webs in the mouth of the tubes to catch unwary victims."

That statement brought her right back to Delia. She'd been an unwary victim. Her murderer might be in the nursery today, maybe even in her tour group. That's what the Sheriff was hoping for. That the murderer would come back. To gloat? To murder someone else.

"Are they easy to grow?" asked the medicinal plant guy.

"Very. Once you've got the perfect place for them. They want full sun, and a special soil mix and wet feet. They can't ever dry out. I grow them on my patio in a container that doesn't have a drain hole. When the leaves turn brown, they're done. You just cut them off. The plants are evergreen around here."

After that they moved on to the Hydrangea garden, which of course held many other plants. Trout lilies were up, but not blooming yet. There were still a few late blooming hellebores, Lenten roses, putting on a show in colors of whites, pinks, cherries, lime greens and maroons. Some were spotted, some doubles. Epimediums with their delicate fairy flowers were peaking. The flowers came in white, yellow, orange, purple, pink, red and scarlet.

And of course, Pulmonaria covered the ground.

"Now these are medicinal. The common name is lungwort. I don't know about their efficacy, but they are an old medicine used to clear the lungs. The leaves are plain green, spotted, striped or streaked with white. The cultivars have different foliage. The predominant flower color is pink with some flowers blue. There are also plain pink or reddish, plain blue and plain white varieties. This plant grows well around here, is slug resistant and stays green throughout the winter. In the late spring, after it's done blooming we'll go through and shear them back and let them grow fresh foliage. Just a lovely plant and it brings such light to our shade gardens."

The medicinal guy didn't take notes on this one. Too

common, Gina decided.

The next garden was the sunny border. It was in an exposed area where the temperatures were cooler. Filled with spring bulbs and flowering shrubs. Delia had limited the Rhododendrons in the garden. Most of them were too dull the rest of the year, but there were six different ones here, in full bloom. The other shrubs, Weigela, Deutzia, Philadelphus, star Magnolia, Pieris and Kalmia, were all putting on a show.

"As you can see this section of the garden is all about the flowers. Later in the season, once the blooming shrubs and bulbs are done, the yellow foliage will be the predominant accent. And the roses will burst on the scene. All the shrubs have Clematis vines growing on them and those will be blooming. The summer perennials will come on in full force."

Melanie's tour group was coming past. Melanie smiled to let her know she was just where she should be. Not taking too long or going too fast.

"This shrublet here is Scutellaria baicalensis. It's an herb from China used for fevers, shingles and the like. In the summer it has lovely purple flowers that look like upward facing Penstemon."

The medicinal guy perked up at that. He wrote down the name, asking her to spell the last part for him. Luckily, she knew how. He seemed to know plants enough to have possibly been involved in the plant theft, possibly the murder.

Gina couldn't keep her focus on the tour. She let people wander for a bit.

Her mind kept rolling back to who killed Delia. What was that saying on all the cop shows? Motive, means and opportunity?

David had the means and opportunity. Perhaps the motive.

If a drug company was involved, they could have sent someone. Could it be Jonathon Ashley? Anyone, even wimpy-looking him, could have wielded the shovel. He could have snuck into the nursery early. Everyone had been so busy, no one would have noticed. He could have smuggled the plants out to his car. Had he acted alone?

Then there was Mark Morris. He could have been jealous of Delia's relationship with Renee. Could also have smuggled the plants out to his car. Since he already had a nursery and plant business, finding the right buyer would be a piece of cake for him. Or perhaps he had help. From one of the staff?

Maybe Karen. Gina hated to think about anyone she knew having the capability to murder, but the Sheriff had said, everyone is a suspect. Karen could definitely heft a shovel. She had been at the nursery when Delia was murdered. Motive? Wanting to get rid of Delia. Maybe buying Renee out and getting the nursery? That was a long shot. Selling the plants, yes, she could do that. Maybe Delia caught her and Karen hadn't planned on that. But selling those three plants might give her enough money to open her own nursery.

Provided Renee was willing to give up the nursery. And what about Renee? That had been a brutal argument, but Renee had been really torn up last night. Gina didn't think she could have killed Delia. But there was motive. She might be really angry about the affair. And it's possible she thought Delia wouldn't have given up about the guy coming into their business. And with Delia dead, Renee could take over the nursery. She'd lose Delia's rising star/plant hunter charisma, but could create her own image. Grieving lover, valiantly carrying on the work all the while making the nursery wildly successful.

Or it could be any combination of the above, working together. One killing Delia, the other stealing plants. Gina shook her head. This was going to drive her crazy, suspecting everyone around her.

"What is that smell?" asked one of her group, dragging Gina back to the present.

"That's the Philadelphus," said Gina. "The common name is

mock orange. All three species here are blooming right now." She pointed to each of the large fifteen foot tall shrubs. The scent was sweet and very noticeable. She breathed it in.

They moved on to the Japanese, Chinese and Vietnamese Gardens. The gardens were designed in a Pacific Northwest style, but each garden held plants primarily from each of those regions. The exceptions were the massive cedar, fir, hemlock or maple trees, which were natives. Delia had been unwilling to remove large, healthy trees and the gardens were all the better for it. They had a mature feeling, even though many of them were less than a decade old.

They crossed paths with Brianna's group at that point.

Lastly, the tour walked through the kitchen garden, filled with herbs and salad greens right now. There were carrots, leeks, asparagus and garlic. Nursery employees had cleared the spaces where tomatoes, pumpkins, zucchini, eggplant and cucumbers would go. All the heat lovers. The raised beds were built in a Celtic knot pattern. It was a very formal and beautiful kitchen garden.

In the center stood a massive blue urn, overflowing with water which recycled itself with a pump. Hummingbirds splashed through the fountain in the center, clicking warnings at each other to stay out of their territory.

The tour group was enchanted. None of this group were locals and many had never seen a hummingbird before.

Flopsy, the nursery's black and white long-haired cat, named for his ragged flopping ear, sat on the edge of one of the beds, accepting pets, but not distracted from his mission of watching the hummingbirds. Just in case one should stray within reach.

They moved on to the Grassy Garden. Filled with at least fifty species of ornamental grasses and many rock garden plants. The grasses looked good, but put on their main show in late summer when they flowered. At this time of year, they were just returning to life after a long winter. However, this border was situated on the edge of a bluff that overlooked the sound. Since the grasses were still short this early in the season, the view was magnificent.

"Over there is the mainland," Gina said. "And down there, if you squint, you can see Mt. Rainier. It's a bit hazy today. Oh, and down there look, there's a pod of whales. They look like killer whales."

That got the group really excited.

They finished with the formal fruit garden. Apples, pears, cherries and peaches espaliered along brick walls to hold in the heat. There were blackberries and raspberries pruned extensively and trailed along wires. Trellises of two different types of kiwis. Blueberry bushes stood in the center. Several different types of strawberries grew in raised beds and pots. Other containers, which wintered in the greenhouse, held small lemon, lime and orange bushes. At this time of year, the garden still looked fairly bare. The plants here were severely pruned and controlled. Melanie sometimes called it the Tortured Garden, but the fruit output was enormous.

The group ended back at the main part of the nursery at noon.

Gina had been carrying her water bottle on the tour and it was nearly empty. She went into the restroom and refilled it.

When she came out, Melanie was there.

"Better grab lunch now. Another tour at 1."

"Are you eating?"

"In just a minute. Meet you in there."

Gina stood in line, got her sandwich and sat down. She was joined by Sheriff Jansson.

"Good afternoon," she said.

"Good afternoon," he said.

"How's the investigation going?"

"It's humming along. I have some questions for you."

"Hopefully, I have some answers."

"But are they the right ones?" he asked.

She laughed. "Probably not. I've always been too contrary to have the right answers."

"That's a good thing sometimes."

"I tend to remember the times when it wasn't a good thing. Job interviews, weddings, funerals, that sort of thing."

He laughed.

After they got their sandwiches, they sat down.

He asked, "What have you found out?" just as she took a huge bite of her sandwich.

She was starving, having eaten breakfast so early. It took a long time to chew that bite.

"About what?" she finally was able to ask.

"About who the murderer might be?"

"Are you trying to get me to do your job for you?" she asked.

"Nope. I've just noticed that in those cases where someone was murdered and it wasn't random, people who know the victim and their small circle of acquaintances often have insights to offer that wouldn't have occurred to me."

"Ah insights. Well, I do have a couple. No three.

"Okay," Sheriff Jansson said, writing it down in that little notepad he always used.

"David was supposed to fix the water lines for the mist tent on Thursday night. They were clogged. That's why Delia was in there yesterday morning, checking to make sure the cuttings were getting misted."

"Okay," he said.

Gina couldn't tell if he was humoring her.

"And Mark Morris, the one she had an affair with, was here yesterday."

"I knew that, got the photo of him."

"I don't know if he was who Renee and Delia were arguing about about, the fling, and the man who wanted to come in to their business. Not sure if they were talking about one man or two."

"Okay."

"And there was a guy on my tour this morning, Jonathon Ashley. He asked about medicinal plants. A lot. Got me to wondering if he worked for a drug company."

"He still here?"

"I don't know. He might be shopping."

"I'll look into that," the Sheriff said, taking a bite of his sandwich.

"And it occurred to me that it could be any two people who did this. One killing Delia, the other grabbing the plants."

"That's a possibility. Which people?"

"I've got five that come to mind."

"Who?"

Gina took a sip of her water. It was ice cold and fresh tasting. The nursery was on a well and had wonderful tasting water.

"Well, David. Then Karen is a possibility, but I have a hard time visualizing her killing Delia. Mark Morris. Possibly a drug company guy, maybe the one who was on my tour or maybe that's something they would hire out, they've got lots of money. The last possibility is Renee. I have a hard time thinking of her as a murderer as well."

"Those are all good choices. I have a couple of others for you to think about."

"Who?" she asked.

"Tyler Glass."

"Tyler? He's so young. I don't know much about him. Never really spoken to him. He seems polite, but immature. Even for someone in their late teens. Living in his own world. He just graduated, I can't picture him being a murderer either. Who's the other one?"

"Karl Erickman."

"I don't recognize the name," Gina said.

"He owns Bayside Nursery in Seattle. He was here yesterday, shopping. I hear he has a lot of customers who buy extremely rare, one of a kind plants and who are willing to pay the price."

"Interesting. I've got no insight on that one. But you know, Delia and Renee went into Seattle Thursday night to have dinner with some of the Hort Heads in town for the conference. Delia had a tendency to brag about plants that she has and you don't. If she talked about some of the plants that are now missing . . . well you might ask Renee if she did."

"I'll do that," he said.

Melanie plopped down on a chair next to Gina.

"Whew, finally here. I got waylaid by a customer, looking for petunias! As if we had petunias here."

"Wondered what took you so long."

Melanie launched into her sandwich like a starving person.

Gina pulled her phone out and looked at the time.

"How long is lunch?" she asked Melanie.

"Thirty minutes. And two fifteen minute breaks."

"Guess I'd better get back to work," said Gina. She finished the pulled pork sandwich with its snappy sauce.

Just then a Deputy appeared in the tent and waved at the Sheriff. Another Deputy, in a khaki-colored uniform stood farther away, with a German shepherd on a leash. Was he from a different county?

"Oh, the dog's here," said Sheriff Jansson. "We're off to the woods."

He finished his food as well and stood up.

"Not the gardens?"

"Trail doesn't lead that way."

Gina threw her garbage in the trash and went out to the courtyard, looking for Karen.

Was she supposed to lead another tour or help customers find plants this afternoon?

The Sheriff and Deputy wove through the customers, heading back towards the mist greenhouse.

The nursery was jammed with people. Gina finally found Karen helping customers check out plants. She and Tyler were tallying people's boxes of plants. Stacy was ringing them up. Pamela was snapping photos of people with their boxes of plants, chatting them up and basically entertaining everyone while the line moved slowly forward.

Which left Renee, Brianne and David helping people find the plants they were looking for and answering questions. Unless one of them was leading a tour.

"What do you need me to do?" asked Gina.

Karen handed Gina a small pad of paper and a pen.

"Why don't you tally plants for a bit. Just put a hash mark for each plant under the number. If someone brings a plant in that's a different price, just write the price down. If the plant's unpriced, text me the name of it and a dollar sign and I'll give you the price. I'm going to make sure the greenhouse people get lunch breaks."

"You're going to take a break too, right?"

"I'll do it when everyone else is done. If Renee ever shows up. Oh, and the next tour's scheduled for 2:30PM. Hope we can pry people away to lead them."

Gina spend the next two hours writing hash marks and admiring people's plants. The one thing about nearly all the plant people was that they were patiently standing in line, and friendly. She had enough retail experience to know that was unusual. For plant people, the rush was to actually find all the plants they were looking for in the nursery. Once they'd gotten their box or cart filled, they were generally patient about waiting to pay because they had plenty of plants to stand and admire and plan where to put them when they got home.

The Sheriff, Deputy and police dog wandered through the nursery several times. Gina was tallying plants in the covered area just outside the store. Once tallied, the person would leave their box of plants on the rack and take their paper into the store to pay. Then return with a receipt and collect their box.

So she had a good view of the Sheriff. He was looking at everyone. Not missing a thing. At one point, the dog started to lunge at someone who had their back to Gina. The Deputy pulled on the dog, forcing him to sit. But the dog still barked and stared at the man.

Sheriff Jansson went up to the man, who was looking at a display of plants. They talked for a bit and Sheriff Jansson showed the man his badge. They ended up walking out to the parking lot together.

A chill went up Gina's spine as she saw it was Jonathon Ashley.

She kept working.

Pamela was talking to one man for a long time, flirting with him. He was probably in his forties, well dressed in a pair of tight jeans, a short sleeved tailored shirt with a botanical print on it. He wore very stylish black shoes. His hair was short and he had a trimmed beard, mustache and soul patch. He wore an elaborate ring on his third finger. Strands of gold, silver and copper woven together, a very pricey item. Tiny gold hoops shone from both ears.

He was definitely flirting back, but it was apparent to Gina that he simply liked flirting. With everyone, men and women.

She glanced at his name tag when she tallied up his box. Karl Erickman. The nursery owner who the Sheriff was talking about.

"You have a lot of very nice plants here," said Gina.

"I know. I'm so glad I found this one," he said, touching what looked like a stick just beginning to leaf out with blackish leaves. "It's all the rage in England. Impossible to find over here still."

Gina read the tag, Cotinus coggygria 'Black Death'. A smoke tree with blue-black leaves.

"Nice," she said.

"I got the last one, Renee said. It's going to be glorious."

"Have you got a spot picked out for it?"

"I'm going to put it in a container for a few years, let it grow up. Then put it in a black and chartreuse bed."

"Great drama," said Gina.

He smiled at her with a grin that spoke of avarice.

She returned his smile and handed him the tally sheet. It was the largest one she'd done so far. Stacy would add everything up on the cash register but Gina guessed the man had over $600.00 in those boxes. And he'd been here yesterday shopping. He must have a lot of money. Even his clothes and appearance spoke of money.

Although most of what he'd bought today would have to be grown on if he was planning on reselling them at his nursery. Ravenswood Nursery did most of their business by mail order and plants had to be small enough to ship. She guessed that most of them were for his personal use.

He went into the office to pay and Gina took a deep breath and let it out. She hadn't even realized she'd been holding it.

All of these possible murderers hanging around made her feel edgy. How was it that she'd gotten roped into helping at the nursery? She'd just pitched in. To help Melanie, mostly.

By the time the day ended her feet hurt again and she felt exhausted.

She went out to her car and drove home. Fed the cats, microwaved a frozen enchilada dinner and sat with her feet up while she ate and drank a bottle of amber ale. She watched the news. Delia's death made the Seattle news. They even interviewed Sheriff Jansson.

"We have a suspect in custody, but the investigation is ongoing."

The camera showed some footage of the nursery and mentioned the conference that was going on. Then a commercial came on.

Gina just sat there with her mouth open. Who did they have in custody?

"Please let it be a complete stranger."

It must be a slow news day for a Seattle station to cover a

murder that happened an hour and a half away. Then again Delia was well known, even outside hard core plant people.

Gina went to bed early feeling despondent.

She needed to get up and go paint again before working at the nursery, which was the last place she wanted to be.

How was Renee coping? Gina had barely seen her today with all the customers. She should make a point of seeking her out tomorrow. See if there was anything she could do. Bring her dinner, or something.

A lot of people had helped her in all sorts of ways when Ewan died. She should pass the kindness on.

Tomorrow, she'd find time to seek out Renee and talk to her.

DAY 3 - SUNDAY

Sunday she arrived at the nursery at nine. That gave her an hour to paint before the nursery opened. Sundays the open hours were ten to five. Later in the summer, as daylight hours extended, they'd be open till six.

It had rained the night before and the air smelled fresh and clean as she walked across the gravel parking lot. There were two police cars there, a Deputy's sedan and the Sheriff's SUV.

She found both of them in the outside dining area, drinking coffee from a local espresso stand and talking to Karen.

Gina waved as she passed by.

"Gina, could you come here?" asked Karen.

She walked towards them.

"Painting again?" asked the Sheriff.

"Yes, is that a problem?"

"No, just curious." he said.

Karen said, "They're arrested someone, but they're not a hundred percent sure he's involved. Just thought you should know."

"Who did you arrest?"

"Jonathon Ashley."

"Why did you arrest him if you're not sure he's the one."

"To see what birds get flushed out of the underbrush," said Sheriff Jansson. "This goes no further than the two of you, understand."

"Yes," said Gina. "So did the police dog tell you anything yesterday?"

"We're not sure," he said.

Gina had the feeling that he knew things, but wasn't telling.

"Okay, anything else? I've only got an hour to paint."

"Nope, we're done here," said the Sheriff.

"Today should be a tiny bit less crazy," said Karen. "I think yesterday was our largest customer day for the conference."

"Well, I'm ready for whatever happens."

With that she walked to the tropical greenhouse and set up. She finished all the detail work on the orchid and then it was time to clean up. She took the completed painting and her bag out to her car and then returned to the courtyard.

The parking lot was already full and customers were standing around, waiting for word that the nursery was open. The morning rush was even larger than yesterday's. Gina took a deep breath.

"Gina, could you help people with plants again this morning? We're only having two tours going out this morning. We were slammed on the nursery end yesterday."

"I'd love to," she said.

Then she was inundated by a whirr of questions, and searching through greenhouses for plants. They were beginning to sell out of the most trendy plants as well as anything with a flower on it. Plant nerds said it was all about the foliage, but they were suckers for blossoms too.

All the squatting and trying to read tiny print on the tags, lifting and standing was taking its toll on her body. Tonight she'd take a long hot bath, with epsom salts. And go to bed early. The cats would appreciate that.

Halfway through the morning she heard several screams come from the garden. Her heart sank. She hoped someone had probably stumbled on the remains of one of Maisie or Flopsy's half-eaten meals.

Last year wild rabbits had moved into the area, Melanie told her. The resident cats had grown fond of rabbit, but they always left behind the uneaten stomach and a few other organs. It was fairly gross.

But no, even pieces of dead rabbit would rate just one scream, not several.

She moved off towards the garden, in the direction of the screams and was almost mowed down by Sheriff Jansson and a Deputy running past.

"Sorry," yelled the Deputy.

They were heading off towards the garden.

What now?

Gina kept walking as fast as she could, running wasn't something she could do anymore. By the time she got out to the garden, the Deputy was herding people out of the area.

Karen was leading a tour group back to the nursery and her face looked white and pinched.

She met her eyes and for a second, Gina saw a look of sheer panic crossed Karen's face. Then it was gone as Karen moved off, followed by the crowd.

Gina tried to see around the Deputy, but there was so much foliage, she couldn't even see the Sheriff.

"I'm sorry Ma'am. We're closing the garden. You'll have to go back."

"What happened?" asked Gina.

"I don't know."

Gina returned to the nursery, which was now swamped with people. She continued to help customers. She was working with Brianna and David. The three of them could barely keep up with the customers' demands. It was almost a relief to be so busy that worrying was shoved to the back of her brain for an hour or two.

Gina felt exhausted. She was looking forward to Tuesday and staying home with her feet up and not worrying about murders.

Lunch didn't happen until two in the afternoon. Karen came to relieve her. Gina noticed her eyes were red, as if from crying.

"Are you okay?"

"I'm okay. Grab your lunch and then come back and let Brianna go eat."

Gina walked away, realizing that Karen was shaking. With anger or grief she couldn't tell. Maybe the reality of Delia's death had finally hit her.

As Gina walked past the entrance to the gardens she noticed crime scene tape across the path tied between two shrubs. What had happened? Had a customer been murdered?

That the Sheriff was here didn't make her feel any safer.

She peered into the store. Stacy was cashiering. Outside Tyler was tallying people's boxes of plants. Pamela was taking photos and gabbing with people. The lines were long.

Gina went into the dining area. All the seats were taken. That was okay, she'd go eat in her car, or maybe the gardens. The line to get food was long too.

She ordered the beef brisket sandwich today. And grabbed a bottle of iced tea.

By the time she got her sandwich, Gina figured there was only about fifteen minutes left of her lunch half hour. Although she hadn't taken a morning break.

She headed out through the vegetable garden, which enabled her to skirt the crime scene tape. And no one took this route out to the gardens, so they were empty. All the customers were shopping or eating.

She took a small unused path that would take her to the shady woodland garden. She wanted to see what the crime scene tape was all about. They must have found something that told them who killed Delia.

It was nearly silent here. Still, voices from the entire morning echoed in her head, all jumbled up. She was used to spending most of her time alone. Being around all these people was exhausting.

The beef in her sandwich was tender and spicy, lots of chilies. She was grateful for the iced tea, to cool off her mouth. she ate while walking through the garden. It was an attempt to casually make her way to where the detectives were.

She wanted to know what happened, yet she didn't want to know. Until she found out, Gina wouldn't be able to concentrate on anything. She was so afraid someone else had been murdered. She hoped it was something else.

But why would someone scream more than once?

Yesterday's warm weather had brought the spring plants to an exploding point. Flowers were bursting out everywhere. It looked like the hydrangeas were coming in early too. Two days of warm weather and several more had opened their blue, white, green or rose colored blooms.

Using small working paths, not the main walkways through the gardens, she got to the shade garden before she spotted a Deputy. He was walking around the garden bed, eyes down toward the ground, looking for something.

Delia would have been horrified to see someone other than staff walking in her garden beds.

Gina skirted around to the left on the working path and was hidden by a cluster of spiky mahonia and conifers.

On the other side of the hill stood Sheriff Janssen and another Deputy. The Deputy was searching for something on the ground. Sheriff Janssen stood on the main walkway, talking to someone wearing a white coverall who squatted on the ground.

She stood silently and listened to their conversation.

"My best guess is that she was killed by the garden spade. Immediately. I'll know more once I've got her on the table."

"Thanks Doc. Can you tell me the time of death?"

"Not long before you called me. I'm guessing ten, ten-thirty."

"Okay, you can take the body away. We'll need to look under it."

"I'll call the ambulance then."

Gina decided it was time to move out in the open. She couldn't learn anything else from here.

She needed to see who'd been killed. It had to have been the same murderer. Garden spade? Delia had been killed by a shovel. The killer was using whatever was handy.

She moved out from behind the evergreens, intently sipping her ice tea and looking at a huge specimen of Paeonia lutea 'Ludlowii' that stood twelve feet tall and was bursting with lemon yellow flowers.

"Excuse me, no one's allowed out in the gardens now Miss," said Sheriff Janssen.

Gina turned to him.

"Oh, it's you Gina. I'm sorry, we've closed the gardens."

"Oh, I'm sorry. I didn't know."

"How did you get out here?"

"I came out through the kitchen garden, since all my normal dining places were full. I thought I'd come check out this glorious peony. What's happened?" she asked.

"There's been another murder."

"Who, if I may ask?"

"You can ask."

Gina just looked at him, trying to decide if she should use the *'I'm as sweet as apple pie'* look or the withering *'Don't you dare empty that bottle of orange juice on the carpet'* look.

Sheriff Janssen said, "It's Renee. Renee's dead."

"What? Oh my," said Gina. She put the hand with the iced tea out to steady herself against a massive cedar trunk. She felt overwhelmed with sadness. Wiping the hot tears running down her face, she asked, "Is it the same murderer?"

"Looks like it. You can't tell anyone."

"Not even Karen? She'll need to decide what to do with the nursery. This isn't a business that can just close down, like a, a, a bank. Someone has to be here and take care of things."

"Karen already knows. So does Melanie. I've sworn them to secrecy. No one else can know, until I tell them. No one. Understand?"

"Yes. I do. This is terrible. First Delia and now Renee. Who could have done such a thing?" Her tears wouldn't stop. Not used to crying in front of people, she wiped her face with the back of the hand holding the remaining sandwich. Which she certainly didn't feel like eating anymore.

"I don't know," said Sheriff Janssen. "But we will find out."

"I should probably get back. Go back to work, so Brianna can take a lunch. We should just close the nursery. But we can't do that until everyone knows though, can we?"

"Just finish out the rest of the day if you can. Act normally. If someone asks, tell them you've heard some bad news about a relative's health or something. I'll talk to Karen at the end of the day. We'll see how things stand then."

"Do you think anyone else is in danger?"

"I don't know. Probably not today, at least."

She nodded. "Should I go back the way I came?"

"This way's faster," he said, pointing down the main path.

"Okay, I don't want to mess up your crime scene," she said. "I want this bastard caught."

"So do we."

She walked past him and headed back towards the main nursery, trying to keep from crying. Then she remembered Karen, just before she let Gina go to lunch. That's why she'd seemed so upset.

Gina swallowed the last of her ice tea, which was now warm.

She shoved the bottle and the rest of her sandwich in the trash container at the end of the path. Just next to the crime scene tape. She wiped her hands on the back of her hoody, grateful for its dark coloring. Then wiped her eyes again and took a deep breath.

She went to the greenhouses and found Brianna helping a woman.

"I'm relieving you, go eat."

"I'll finish this first."

"No, you go eat. Now, your baby needs food and you need to sit down."

Brianna looked sort of relieved.

Gina helped the woman find the Hydrangea variety she was looking for. Gina even pointed one plant out that had buds on it.

"Oh, it's going to bloom this summer."

"Wonderful, I can hardly wait!"

The woman went off with her box, in seventh heaven.

A while later, she saw Karl Erickman again. He was flirting with an Englishman. Who turned out to be Mark Morris when she could finally see his conference badge. They were having a discussion about some plant.

Gina watched them while fussing with a flat of plants, setting them all upright again and arranging them neatly. Were either or both of them the murderers? She made herself relax, calm down and listen to their conversation.

"They're just so common now," said Karl Erickman. "Even my neighbor has them."

"I adore them. I don't care who has them. They'll never go out of style for me," said Mark Morris.

"What is it you see in them?"

"The evergreen leaves, the delicate fairy flowers, the range of color. They grow in dry shade. They're just excellent plants. They fit in everywhere, beneath shrubs, beneath your tall cedars here."

"I just can't like them. Their leaf texture is dull, they always look dead. They bloom for such a short time and in March, when no one in their right minds is out in the rain. You have to cut back the leaves to see the tiny flowers. Just awful."

"You like big, brassy things don't you? Most Americans tend that direction, I've noticed."

"And you English with your itsy-bitsy flowers, where you have to get half a million blooms just to make a show. It's all too fussy for me."

They both laughed and headed off to argue about something else. So that had been Delia's fling. He was good looking, although a bit on the arrogant side. But then Delia had been, too. Everything centered around her and the nursery.

Melanie came up to her. "We are totally sold out of all Polygonatum."

"Good, cause I'm clueless about what they are. My brain is just fried today."

"Solomon's Seal is a Polygonatum. We just carry fancier ones here."

"Okay, I'll try to remember that. Have you had lunch yet?"

"No, I'm waiting for Brianna to get back."

"We're only taking lunch breaks one at a time today?"

"Today, yup. Shorthanded. And we have an abundance of customers."

They were interrupted by another wave of people arriving. It was a grueling day and Gina was relieved when five o'clock came.

"Go home," Karen told Gina.

"There are still customers here."

"Stacy's ringing the bell in a minute."

Just then the deep gong sounded throughout the whole nursery. She felt the vibration in her chest.

"Go, while you can."

Gina wanted to talk to Karen, but Karen shooed her off. So she slipped out of her hoodie and folded it up, trying to look like another customer in order to leave invisibly.

She waved at Melanie, who was involved with customers. Melanie just nodded.

In the parking lot, she was struck by the many police vehicles. Not all of them from Island County – Raven Island Police. Some were Snohomish County vehicles, others Stanwood Police.

One of the Raven Island deputies was standing by his car, talking on his radio. She recognized him from the last two days. He was tall, with a blond crew cut. Sort of beefy looking. When he stopped talking, she went up to him. The nameplate on his pocket read Deputy Allen Hofsteader.

"Hi, I'm Gina. I've been working here. Has something else happened?"

"I can't tell you Ma'am," said the young man. "We're still investigating."

"I understand, thanks." She was turning to walk away.

"You're the artist."

"Yes, I am. Although I've been helping in the nursery because they're so overwhelmed."

He looked like he was thinking.

"Are you coming back to work tomorrow?"

"No one's made an announcement that we're closed tomorrow. It's the last day of the conference. I guess if I don't hear anything I'll just show up. I'm sure the customers will too."

"That is a problem. I'll remind the Sheriff about potential customer tomorrow. It's his call of course."

"Well thank you. I appreciate all your hard work. I hope you catch the murderer."

"So do we Ma'am. So do we."

Gina got in her car and drove home.

At home she called Melanie, but only got her voicemail.

"Hi. Call and let me know what's happening, please."

She kicked her shoes off in the entryway and was immediately surrounded by purring and meowing cats.

"Oh hello kids. Dinnertime is it?"

The meowing said yes.

After dinner, she was tempted to go straight to bed. But instead, drew a hot bath with epsom salts and rose oil. At the last minute, she lit a few candles and turned the lights out. Then she crawled into the hot water, making sure her cell phone was within reach.

The heat felt wonderful on her aching muscles, and they were all aching.

She'd only been soaking a few minutes when Melanie returned her call. Gina felt relieved, she needed to talk about things.

"How did you know something was happening?" she asked.

"Lots more police, the garden roped off after someone had been screaming out there. And I walked through the garden during my lunch. Ran into Sheriff Janssen."

"Huh. Well, there's more bad news. I only know about Renee cause a woman on one of my tours discovered her body."

"What?" asked Gina.

"We were in the shade garden, the part that's filled with sword ferns and lots of other shrubbery. And the woman saw a rubber boot sticking out of a fern. She looked closer and then screamed. I dove into the bushes to see what was wrong. And there was Renee, hit over the head, and one of those heavy duty garden spades nearby, all bloody. I got everyone out of there and called Karen. Had her go get the Sheriff. It was such a mess."

"Oh, I'm so sorry you had to go through that."

"The worst part was trying to calm the customer down. Most people hadn't seen anything, so I tried to separate the woman from all but her two friends. Karen came and took the rest of the tour group away, while I stayed with them and waited for the Sheriff. I knew he'd want to talk to her and at least he'd have a clue how to calm her down. And maybe me too."

"Who could have killed Renee?"

"Obviously it's more complicated than Renee killing Delia. She still could have, but then who killed her?"

"Is the nursery open tomorrow?" asked Gina.

"I haven't heard that it's not," said Melanie. "Karen wouldn't close it, if it was left up to her. Wouldn't want to give the murderer the satisfaction. She's pigheaded that way. Then again, it's not up to her, is it?"

"A deputy told me it might not be. And really, two people have been murdered. The owners. Shouldn't we just close?"

Melanie didn't answer for a while. Then she said, "I don't know. Someone's going to inherit. They'll want a viable business. I mean, I see your point about closing, but also tomorrow's the last day of the conference. There will still be some first-timers there, who've saved the best for last. And somebody's got to keep watering plants in the greenhouses and then the gardens. Keep the pests under control and weed. If not, then what was the point? There's all these baby plants in the greenhouses, just waiting for someone to care for them so they can fulfill their potential. Delia and Renee would have seen that. They wouldn't have wanted us to close the nursery. They spent the last ten years giving everything they had to make it a success."

"Okay. Well, I'll be there."

"Are you going in early to paint?"

"Are there any flowers left to paint or did you sell them all today?"

"There's an amazing ginger in the tropical house that's all budded out. I thought it would be open today. So probably tomorrow. It would be perfect for your May Day Show."

"Okay, I'll go in an hour early. I gotta get those paintings done. My feet are killing me."

"Yeah, mine too. I've got my shoes off and feet up. Do I hear water?"

"I'm in the tub. Me and my epsom salts."

"Good idea. Maybe I'll do a foot bath before bed. I've got

some epsom salts somewhere. It's been a long week. Want to go out for dinner tomorrow? I know I won't have the energy to cook. This whole situation has been so awful and stressful. I'm exhausted. I know I shouldn't feel like that, at least I'm alive."

"It would be nice to go out for dinner. I've run out of instant food here. I need to go shopping. Tuesday. Or maybe Wednesday. And yes, we're alive, that's something to be grateful for. We can't do anything about Delia and Renee. Our feeling awful won't help them."

"You always have such common sense. Okay, I'll see you when I get there tomorrow."

"Deal," said Gina.

The water was getting cold, so she got out of the tub.

In bed she lay awake for quite a while, her mind unwilling to stop turning the problem around.

Who would have wanted to murder Renee? She wasn't the kindest, gentlest person, but she was always fair.

Had Renee found out who killed Delia and confronted them? Or was the person afraid they'd been seen by her? With both Delia and Renee gone, what would happen with Ravenswood? Did either of them have wills?

She rolled and tossed, finally getting to sleep in the wee hours.

DAY 4 - MONDAY

Half an hour before her alarm went off Gina was wakened by the thundering herd. Alice and Albert were chasing each other around, under and over the bed. Their pre-feeding play ritual.

"You two are really annoying this morning. Go away." She stuffed a pillow over her head, but the cats continued to bounce on and off the bed, playing tag.

She was not going to be able to get back to sleep.

Gina groaned and pulled herself out of bed.

"Tonight you two are sleeping on the couch."

She fed the monsters and then made coffee. At least she didn't hurt as much this morning. Thank goodness for epsom salts.

Gina dressed and ate a breakfast of bacon, eggs over easy and toast.

She'd just finished washing up when the phone rang.

"Hello."

"Mom, it's me."

"Joanna, how are you?"

"Good. I've been calling, but you didn't answer."

"Oh my goodness, I've been so busy I haven't checked my messages for days."

"What have you been doing?"

Gina filled her in about working at the nursery and about the entire conference coming out to the nursery. She left out the part about the murders. Joanna would just worry.

"Are you all right financially?"

"Oh dear yes. Ewan and I saved a lot when we both worked. Selling the old house paid for this house and a bit more. I just helped out because they were short-handed and so obviously needed another body, short term. Today's the last day of the conference, so I'm done. It's been fun meeting everyone, but I've got paintings to do."

"Good, I'm glad everything's okay. When is your gallery show again?"

"May day."

"Oh, how perfect. Tom has a meeting in Seattle on the second. I thought I might come out with him. I've got loads of vacation time."

"It would be wonderful to see you. If you want to stay here, I've got an extra bedroom. I know it's a ways from Seattle. An hour and a half on a good day, but you're welcome here."

"Thanks. I'll try to firm up our plans. Does the ferry run regularly?"

"Oh honey, there's no ferry. There's a bridge. You can drive to Seattle."

"Really? Wow, I thought there'd be a ferry since you're on an island. I guess I remember all those ferry rides we went on when I was a kid."

"We could find a ferry to go on, if you feel the need," said Gina.

"I'll think about that."

"I think I'll be tied up until the show opens, but after that my time will be my own again. Stay as long as you like and we can go off and have fun together."

"That's just what I need! Thanks Mom. I'll call when I have the flights and all of Tom's information. I've got to get back to work."

"Looking forward to seeing you. I love you, dear. And say hello to Tom."

"I will. Love you too, Mom. Bye."

Gina hurried and gathered up her things and left the house, her spirits lifted by the phone call. She was going to get to see one of her daughters. What fun they would have together.

At the nursery, there were three police vehicles, as well as Karen's pickup. Two Island County – Raven Island Police and one Stanwood Police.

Gina got her art bag and thermos of coffee and headed back towards the tropical greenhouse. She didn't see or hear anyone.

She dithered over whether she should just walk quietly to the greenhouse and begin painting or let people, especially armed people, know she was there. She decided on the latter.

"Hello," she called. "Karen?"

No response.

"Karen?" she yelled.

"Coming!"

"No need. I just wanted to let you know I'm here. Tropical Greenhouse," yelled Gina.

"Okay."

Gina entered the Greenhouse. It seemed really warm this morning. Some of the plants looked a bit wilted. Had anyone been watering here? She should ask Karen today.

Maisie and Flopsy were stretched out on adjacent benches, basking in the heat. They looked up half-heartedly when she came in, then went back to sleep.

"Well, hello to you too. I'm guessing you both got some food last night or this morning, or you'd be letting someone know about it. I'll have to ask Karen who's taking care of Max. All of you are orphans now, poor kids."

She petted the two cats and they lay there purring as they napped.

She pulled the hoody off. It was far too hot in here to wear that.

Gina set up her painting supplies by the gingers. Two of them were in bloom. The tag for one said it was a spicily-fragrant, red torch ginger. The shape reminded her more of a Dahlia than a torch, but then it was just beginning to bloom. It might look more torch-like when it was fully open.

The other was a shell ginger. It looked sort of like a drooping Gladiolus. The buds, white with pink tips, opened into fragrant, snapdragon-like flowers of yellow, white and pink. The pendulous racemes of flowers were at least eight inches long. As a bonus the variegated green leaves were streaked with a cream color.

Gina made a wash of colors for each one. Then took photographs of them with her camera, so she could paint the details in at home if she had to. She always preferred to paint in person, but would the nursery even be open after today?

By the time she'd finished both washes, it was time to pack up and let them dry. She petted the cats again and hauled everything back to her car. She lay the paintings out on the back seat to dry, finished the last of the coffee in her thermos and headed back to the courtyard. Customers' cars were beginning to trickle into the parking lot. It was already warm enough that she didn't want to wear the hoody. She tied it around her waist in case she needed it later.

She noticed one of the tree peonies was beginning to open. It was a lovely coral pink. She went over and sniffed it. It wasn't exactly sweet, more of a yeasty scent, plus she got a nose full of rain water too.

In the courtyard, customers were lining up.

"Excuse me," Gina said, squeezing through the crowds. People gave her dirty looks until they saw her hoody and realized she was staff. Then they let her through.

Gina joined Karen, Melanie and the rest of the staff in the outside dining area.

They all looked tired, Karen more so than the others.

"Okay, we're all here. As many of you know, Renee was killed the night before last. The Sheriff's Department hasn't told us anything about what's going on, only that we could open the gardens today. I don't know what will happen to the nursery. Wish I did. I do know you'll all get paid and that we'll continue to be open until someone, either the Sheriff or Margaret, the bookkeeper, tells us we need to close. That includes tomorrow, because we've got watering and mail order and propagating to catch up on. But today's the last day of the conference. For a lot of people, this will be their first visit to the nursery. Let's make it great."

Brianna asked, "What do we tell people who ask about Renee? A lot of people were here yesterday and they'll be gossiping."

"Tell them that both Delia and Renee are dead, and that we're all heartbroken. It's the truth and they'll find out soon enough anyway. We don't know who did it, the police are still investigating."

"Shall we open the gates?" asked Stacy.

"Go for it," said Karen.

Gina told Karen about the topical greenhouse needing watering.

Karen said, "I'll make sure to hit that tonight before I close up."

"Oh, and is someone taking care of Max? And the cats?"

"I took Max home with me last night. Poor guy, he's been cooped up in their house all weekend because of the investigation. I've got a fenced yard and Jack, my dog, was so excited to have company. The two became fast friends and played last night till they were exhausted. I fed the cats this morning. They're pretty self-maintaining, thank goodness."

"I'm so glad. I was worried about Max being stuck in their house all alone. What do you want me to do today?"

"Can you lead a tour? I don't think I can face going out in the garden again today. Melanie can't either."

"I'm fine with doing that," said Gina.

So Gina, Brianna and David divided up the tour groups. They asked people who burned to know all the plant names to go with Brianna and David. Those who were looking for creative inspiration to go with Gina.

The crowds divided themselves neatly into three groups.

Gina spent three hours in the garden. Her group was thrilled to hear her critique of the gardens, what was working, what needed changing.

She was surprised to see no sign of the Sheriff. No crime scene tape. No deputies lurking about. Maybe they were all over at Delia and Renee's house. Or perhaps they were in the mist tent greenhouse, but she thought they would have gotten all the information they needed from there by now. Unless something had changed. Someone could have gotten in there since the murder and gone through Delia's collection of plants. Goodness knows, they were short-handed enough staff-wise. No one would have noticed till much later.

Her mind had all sorts of imaginary ifs that could be happening.

It was after one in the afternoon when she made it back to the main nursery. Her group had lots and lots of design questions. Gina was far from an expert on garden design, but she knew what she liked and had a good grasp of many of the current styles. Melanie was always dragging her off to tour gardens.

Gina's garden was tiny in comparison to most. Just a couple of beds off the back patio which fronted 'the woods'. Those she left alone. And another narrow bed in front that bordered the edge of the house and carport on one side and the rose, gray and white pavers on the other. Just room for a few short shrubs and perennials. Her garden was low maintenance. Just like she wanted it. Most of gardening was cleaning and she'd had her fill of that with the huge house and garden in Seattle. Cleaning was overrated.

She stood in line for lunch, deciding to get the beef again. And a water. She'd had enough caffeine for the day.

She sat down next to the Sheriff and across from Brianna.

Brianna, as usual, was talking about her plans for the baby's nursery. Gina couldn't blame her. It was common to be preoccupied about being pregnant. And an easier topic than murder.

The Sheriff asked polite questions, and then after while asked Gina how her day was going.

"Good. I led a tour of people who were actually more interested in garden design than individual plants. I actually had something to say."

"And did you get any painting done this morning?"

"I started two more."

"How many more do you need to paint in the next two weeks?"

"I've been afraid to count. I'll do that tomorrow, when I have time to do something about it other than worry. But actually, it's only one week. The following week I have to frame all of them."

"You frame them yourself?"

"I do. That way I know each painting gets the frame it needs. I collect frames from secondhand shops, and buy others when I need them."

"That's clever."

"It's just hard to find ornate frames at the framing shops. They're not in style these days, but sometimes that's what suits the painting."

Brianna finished her lunch and said, "Time for me to get back."

"See you later," said Gina.

"It was nice talking to you," said the Sheriff.

"She's a sweet girl," said Gina.

"That she is. Reminds me of my daughter when she was that age. And she was pregnant at that age too."

"So, you're a grandfather?"

"I am. Three grandkids. Two girls and a boy. They're all great. And you?"

"Not yet. None of my three girls are ready for that yet. One's still touring the world every chance she gets. Another's in a high-paying, grueling job. The other's busy being a mask-maker in Hollywood. I doubt she'll ever settle down. Good thing I'm not living vicariously through them, hoping for grandchildren."

He laughed.

"So, are you any closer to finding out who the murderer is?"

"We've plenty of suspects, but nothing firm yet."

"Did either Gina or Renee have a will?"

"We're looking for that now," he said.

"I don't envy you your job," she said.

"Why?"

"It must be like trying to find a needle in a haystack."

"Not that bad," he said. "Not usually."

"Do you know why this person killed both of them?"

"When I know that, I'll probably know who."

"You said the other day that you arrested the guy to flush someone out. Did it work?"

"Well, he does work for a drug company. Delia had contacted them and he claims to have come here hoping to see the plant, only to find out Delia had been murdered. He was very upset to find out the plant had been stolen. He willingly went through the photos of people who were at the nursery for the last three days. He pointed out two people of interest who had worked for his company and for their competitors, companies where he'd also worked in the past. It seems like there's a cutthroat business of developing new medicines through plant extracts. That means trying out new plants."

"Have you talked to either of those people?"

"One of them. She's been touring all the other gardens for the last three days and very visibly socializing with friends in Seattle. Nearly all her time is accounted for."

"But you haven't talked to the other person?"

"Not yet. I'm waiting to see if he'll show up today."

"Has he been here the other days."

"Yes, he has."

"Might he be mentioned in the will?" she asked.

"That would make a neat and tidy case, wouldn't it?"

"But life's not like that, is it?"

"Rarely. Although sometimes criminals can be incredibly stupid about certain things."

She sipped her water in an attempt to drown some of the flames in her mouth from the beef. Tomorrow she was having food that wasn't spicy. She should probably have gotten a soda.

"I should probably go find out what I'm doing next," she said.

"I thought the crowds were supposed to be less today," he said.

"Has it been crowded? I've been out in the garden."

"It seems more crowded than yesterday. People seem to be buying like crazy."

"They're afraid the nursery's going to close. So they're buying everything they might ever want. Just in case they can't find it elsewhere. Delia carried a lot of plants that no one else did. And she propagated them to spread them around. But most of those who bought them haven't had time to grow them on and do the same. It's going to be such a loss to the gardening community, her being gone."

He asked, "Is the nursery going to close?"

"I have no idea. Depends on the will doesn't it? I heard Renee had completely and irrevocably cut ties with her awful family. Gotten rid of everything that connected her to them. Documents, photos, burned everything and began anew, a couple of decades ago at least. I don't know if Delia had any family. The two of them didn't have kids. So even if they had a will, who would they have left the nursery to?"

"And if they didn't have a will? What a mess that could turn out. The whole thing would go to the state, who would then sell it. Do Karen or any of the other employees have enough money to buy the nursery?" the Sheriff asked.

"I doubt it. I know buying a nursery has always been in Karen's plans, but I'm guessing she hasn't got enough. Nursery work doesn't pay a lot. Delia got her money from teaching in Horticultural Programs. And a couple of savvy deals with selling medicinal plants that turned into gold mines for Big Pharma. I don't think any of the other employees would want to buy it, even if they had the money."

"Interesting."

"Is it?"

"Well, that would say Delia already had a relationship with the drug companies. It would narrow our search down. Where would the papers be for those?"

"I don't know. Karen might. That was over a decade ago. The correspondence might have been through email. Or it might have been all done by mail or phone. How far back do phone records go?"

"Depends on if Delia changed numbers and carriers. How long did she live on Raven Island?"

"Just since they bought the nursery, I think. So, a decade."

"And before that?"

"You'd have to ask Karen. Or maybe Melanie. Or any of the knowledgeable plant people here. I know Delia taught right up until they bought the nursery, but I don't know where."

"Thank you. You've been a great help."

"I've just made things more muddled haven't I?"

"No," he said. "You've helped clarify things for me. Really."

"Well, I'd better get back to the fray," she said, draining her water.

"Will you be here tomorrow?"

"I have at least two paintings to finish up. I'd like to do it soon, but I don't know how I'll feel tomorrow. This standing all day and hefting plants has been hard on my body. I might decide to stay home tomorrow and keep my feet up. And nap. If I do, then I'll be back on Wednesday to paint something."

"I'm afraid we'll still probably be here. Sifting through things over at their house. It's grown easier now that Karen has taken Max home with her. He was too much help."

"Yes, he's just that kind of dog. Wants to help with everything. Well, good luck."

"Thank you," he said.

Gina went to find Karen and ended up tallying up people's plants again. And making note of who was there for the fourth day in a row. Karl Erickman bought a huge number of plants. Ten boxes full.

"It's such a shame about Delia and Renee. I'm gutted. They were such dear friends. What's going to happen to the nursery now?"

"I don't know," said Gina.

"It'll close of course, I mean how could anyone fill Delia's shoes? There are so few people on the planet who were trendsetters like her or who knew as much about plants, and who could run a business, and had all the other skills. Most of the time those things don't overlap. But they did in Delia. And Renee, what a fabulous PR person she was. They made a great team. Have they found the murderer yet?"

"No, they're still investigating."

"I heard plants were stolen."

"I haven't heard that. But then I just stepped in to help because they needed a warm body."

"But you must know plants or they wouldn't have hired you."

"I'm a botanical illustrator."

"Oh, you're the artist. My friend George was on your tour this morning. He said that something you said made him able to re-envision his entire six acre garden, which is a stunning garden already. He went on and on about you."

"Well thank you. I have spent rather a lot of time in this garden thinking about it and being inspired."

"It is a lovely garden. Such wonderful plant choices. What are your favorites?"

"It depends on the day. Today, it's that promiscuous coral-colored tree peony just before you get to the front courtyard." She pointed to a bed across from the office which held the mature tree peony.

"Oh I saw her. She is such a lovely old tart."

Gina finished tallying up his plants and before he went to stand in line to pay, he said, "I'm Karl Erickman." He held out his hand.

She shook it. "Georgina Weatherby."

"I look forward to seeing your paintings."

"There's a May day show at the Mason Gallery in town. If you get back up this way."

"Oh, I think I'll be up this way a lot. I want to make sure this nursery doesn't fall apart. And if it does, I'll be buying a lot of specimen plants from the gardens. Most people would probably just buy the land and clearcut it. There's so many expensive plants here. I'll drop by the show. Is it evening?"

"5 p.m. I think. You might check the gallery's website."

"Mason Gallery." He put a note on his phone. "May day. What a lovely day to choose."

"Yes it is."

He left, and she wanted to go wash her hands, but she began to tally up the next person instead.

A plump woman in a purple hoody said, "I was on your tour too. Thank you. You gave me so many ideas for my garden."

"Well thank you."

"I hope the nursery doesn't close. I'm just getting started on this garden at our new house and there's so many plants I need to get."

"I hope so too," said Gina.

The rest of the day went that way. Lots of condolences.

In between customers her mind wandered. Who would have wanted both Delia and Renee dead? Could it be someone local, as simple as a hate crime? Or was it more involved? Had someone wanted the nursery closed? To buy it, or could it have been a competitor? From what the Sheriff had told her, it was likely to have been drug companies out to steal the plant, and perhaps its secrets? What was it all those cop shows said? Follow the money. The most money wasn't in selling plants to gardeners. It was from Big Pharma. So the chances were really good it was them. They were so crooked to begin with, they'd think nothing of a couple of murders and plant theft.

The day rolled into late afternoon and the crowds thinned. Then it began to drizzle. Then the skies emptied themselves on the nursery. Rain came down so hard for a time, she couldn't see past a dozen feet. The water formed an insular curtain around where she was working.

Gina hadn't brought her raincoat today. She'd been so tired this morning it hadn't even occurred to her. Luckily, the plant tallying area was undercover and only dripped a bit. Still, she began to get cold.

She was fantasizing about hot chocolate when the gong sounded. Five o'clock. The remaining drenched customers came to get their plants tallied up and paid for.

"I thought people were kidding about the rain here," said one man.

"Nope. It'll stop in a while, or at least slow down. Maybe," she said.

"I guess that's why the foliage is so lush. You must never have to water around here."

"Oh we do. In August, September and sometimes October we get less rain than parts of Arizona. It's our drought time."

Another customer said, "Then it's nonstop hauling hoses around to keep all that lush foliage happy."

Gina nodded. "Unless you mulch excessively. Then it's a bit better, but still a lot of hose hauling. And the nursery stock needs watering once, maybe twice a day."

"Wow," he said. "That must be quite a job."

"It does keep several people employed. Job security, you know."

He laughed.

It was six before she got out of there. The sky was back to drizzling again.

Melanie was waiting for her just outside the office. Wearing her raincoat.

"You still want to go eat?" she asked.

"I'm starving," said Gina. "Gotta go feed the cats though."

"I figured. I'll follow you and drive again. Gotta get some gas. Think about what you want to eat."

"Mexican sounds good. How about La Cantina? I could use some of their hot chocolate," said Gina.

"Perfect."

An hour later they were seated in a dimly lit booth in the cozy restaurant. The candle on the table between them flickered until it finally settled into burning strongly.

The smell of cumin, cooked cheese and red sauce filled the air. Gina's stomach growled in response.

"Joanna called this morning. She and Tom might be out here when the May day show is on."

"Oh, that's wonderful! I know you miss her."

A server Gina didn't recognize took their orders and brought them water. The boy was barely out of high school, she guessed.

Gina sipped the ice water and shivered.

"You cold?" asked Melanie.

"I guess I am. And tired. I didn't get much sleep last night. And the air conditioning is on in here. In April."

"I didn't sleep will either. Tomorrow's my day off and I'm looking forward to sleeping in. And being away from the nursery. I've got to get some things planted."

Gina laughed. Melanie had an acre of garden. There was always something that needed planting, or moving or doing. Still, it was a beautiful garden.

"I'm looking forward to putting my feet up. If I get enough sleep tonight and have the energy, I'll go in tomorrow and finish those two paintings. Otherwise, it will be Wednesday."

"Wednesday, I'll have my head down, working. Karen and I talked. We don't know what's going to happen with the nursery, but we sold out of a huge amount of plants. We're short on stock. So, I'm going to be busy propagating for the next several months."

"Isn't it the wrong time of year to do that?"

"All of the early spring bulbs are done and have died back. I'll dig and divide those, and get them started in pots. By the time I finish, it will be time to divide Hostas. And then the early blooming perennials, Irises and so on. I'll find things to fill out our empty holes in the sales greenhouses. I have a feeling the nursery's going to have a busy spring and summer. Karen agrees."

"Even if they find a will, it's going to take some time for it to work it's way through the system. And if they don't, it will take longer, probably."

"Exactly. Margaret, the bookkeeper, told Karen we should continue on with business as usual. That way whoever inherits or buys the nursery will have something. She'll see we all get paid. We'll all be taking on more responsibility until the estate is settled, one way or another."

"That's wonderful. I hope your job continues."

The server brought two steaming mugs of Mexican hot chocolate, spiked with Frangelico to them.

Gina sipped hers. It tasted heavenly. The chocolate perfectly balanced with cinnamon and hazelnut. She felt the hot liquid go down her throat.

Then had another crisp tortilla chip dipped in pico de gallo, heavy on the cilantro which suited her just fine.

She took a deep breath.

"This is wonderful. Just what I needed," Gina said.

"Me too."

They sat in silence for a few minutes, sipping and crunching.

Melanie said, "I think Mark Morris is considering buying Ravenswood."

"Really? From who? No one even knows who owns the nursery now."

"I heard him talking to Karen and David. He was asking a lot of questions that were leading that direction."

"Doesn't he already own a nursery in England?" asked Gina.

Yet he'd wanted to buy in with Delia and Renee. Was he planning on selling the one he already owned?

"He does, it's all mail order though apparently. Very little foot traffic he said, cause he's always traveling and out finding new plants."

"Hm. Interesting."

"Isn't it? I wonder if they told the Sheriff that?" asked Melanie.

"Well, he said they'll still be around for the next couple of days. I hope so. Although I don't know if they have any evidence that points to anyone being the murderer. And what will they do with everyone going back home now that the conference is over? England's a long ways away," said Gina.

"I don't know. I sure hope they find something and soon. It's awful with everything this unsettled. I don't know who to trust. Or who might have wanted the two of them dead enough to kill them. Or why."

Gina was hit with a wave of sadness. What a loss these two women were. She'd miss them. What would they have accomplished if they'd lived longer? No one would ever know now.

The server brought their food.

Gina had ordered a couple of cheese and chicken enchiladas, with refried beans. And guacamole on the side. Melanie had a beef tostada.

Gina cut her enchiladas to let the cheese cool off some. She ate tiny bites of the beans, blowing on them first. La Cantina had the best food.

They took their time eating and talking about their kids. Melanie normally worked three days a week and was looking forward to Sunday when she planned to go visit her daughter and grandchild.

By the time the meal was over, Gina had decided to take Tuesday off and stay home. Except for a quick run to the grocery store. She really did need food.

And she must make decisions about how many more paintings still needed to be finished. And what should the subjects be? It was her first major show. All her other exhibitions had been paintings put up in cafes or displays selling them at holiday markets.

This was important. She needed to show the range of her ability. And if she wanted to sell things, she needed a good selection of subjects.

She should do a couple of paintings that were very simple. More zen-like for those who had that sort of decor. She could paint some bamboo stems. The nursery had some very interesting bamboo varieties. But then those weren't flowers.

Melanie dropped her off at home and Gina went inside, changed into some warm fuzzy pajamas and went to bed looking forward to the day ahead.

Before nine at night.

That was a new one.

DAY 5 - TUESDAY

The next morning she woke up to Albert pawing her nose. She rolled over and he stood on her back, kneading.

That was when Alice started meowing piteously.

Gina got up, her sore feet complaining more loudly than Alice. She fed the cats and went back to bed, sleeping soundly for several more hours.

When she woke again it was after ten. She was pinned down on both sides by the cats. Why was it that fifteen pounds of cat became thirty on top of the blankets. Double that with two of them. She was being held down by sixty pounds of cats.

It took her some time to extricate herself from the sheets, blankets, bedspread and cats. The cats just looked at her, then went back to sleep.

She felt awake, but groggy. It took a few minutes of splashing cold water on her face to gain some clarity.

It was Tuesday. Her day of doing almost nothing.

She made a cup of oolong tea and went to check her messages. Her phone was dead. She'd forgotten to plug it in last night.

As she sipped the tea, she laid out her paintings in her studio. There was the peony, the iris, the Narcissus, the double Hellebore, the orchid, the Hibiscus and the two gingers that she needed to finish.

That made eight. So she needed two more paintings.

She'd go in tomorrow and finish up the two gingers and then decide what she'd paint for the last two. Maybe some other interesting plants would be in bloom by then. Once she had all the paintings, she could start planning frames in earnest.

Gina ate a bowl of granola for breakfast and killed off the carton of milk. It was noon. She should pull herself together and go shopping.

After washing up, she dressed, got the grocery list and headed for the only grocery store on the island. It was warm again today. In the mid sixties. She almost wished she'd worn capris and sandals.

Corr's Grocery was fairly large for an independent grocery store. It rivaled the big chains and was the only grocery store on the island, but she loved it. They had a bakery, plus a fish and meat department. Their produce section focused on organic vegetables and fruits. The store carried items one would normally find in an upscale grocery store in Seattle, which suited her. Gina didn't like to cook, but she liked good food.

Pushing the small cart on the stone tiled floor, she walked down the wide aisles, filled the cart with mostly instant, but healthy food. She hadn't liked cooking since her twenties. And cooking for one person just wasn't fun at all.

She read labels though and stuck to ingredients she understood, trying to get a balance of protein and vegetables. With some fresh bananas and organic grapes. She picked up a few things that would make nice instant lunches to eat at the nursery on days she was painting. There wouldn't be any more of that delicious barbecue, which was probably a good thing.

She did fine finding healthy food, until she got to the bakery.

Where she bought half a chocolate cake. The bakery made wonderful cakes.

Gina was loitering in the book section, trying to decide whether to abandon her current, uninteresting book and pick up a new one or to keep reading and hope for the best.

"Well, your taste runs to Janet Evanovich, does it?"

She turned to see Sheriff Jansson.

"Well hello. I didn't expect to run into you here."

"No one ever does. It's where I catch the real crooks."

She laughed.

"I was nearly out of food. Thought I'd better stock up so I can finish those paintings."

"Good idea. Are you coming to the nursery tomorrow?"

"Yes, I am. I have two more paintings to finish, plus two more that I haven't even begun yet."

"Well good. I'd like to sit down and talk to everyone again and go over the timelines again. I have a few more questions for all of you."

"I'm not sure everyone's working tomorrow though. I think people have staggered days off, during the weekdays. It's the busy season for nurseries, but most of the customers come on weekends."

"Well, it'll be good to talk to some of you without the madness of customers."

"Have you found out anything new?"

"Loads upon load of new things. I've got so much information that I can't narrow things down. It's still early days though."

She had no idea what that meant. It had been five days since Delia was killed. And three days since Renee was murdered. Didn't investigations need to happen at the speed of light before the trail was lost? And by now, many of the conference attendees would have left town.

"Well, I'll be there. Probably not at 8 a.m., though."

"Good, well I better get going. I've got to bring lunch to all those starving deputies."

He walked off. She noticed he had a hand basket filled with pre-made sandwiches, sodas and candy bars.

Gina checked out and drove home. Her cell phone pinged on the way home. A text. She'd look at it when she got home. Just a few minutes away.

She drove into her carport and noticed Melanie's blue pickup parked in front of her house. Melanie got out.

"I was hoping you'd be coming back soon."

"Grocery store run," said Gina, popping the trunk.

Melanie helped her carry stuff in.

After she unlocked the door, Gina asked, "Is everything okay?"

"I've just been thinking and I wanted to talk to someone. Before I talked to the Sheriff tomorrow."

"Speaking of the devil, I just saw him at Corrs'."

"Really?"

"Yup. He was buying lunch for himself and the deputies."

"Interesting."

"Why?"

"I don't know. I just thought they'd all be at the nursery today."

"I remember him saying they were going to be over at the house. But people have got to eat and there's no more barbecue."

"Right," said Melanie.

Gina put the frozen and refrigerated things away.

"Want some coffee? Tea?"

"Tea would be nice. Not black. I've had way too much caffeine in the last four days."

"Me too. I slept forever this morning. It was wonderful."

She put water in the kettle, set it on the burner then turned it on.

Pulling mugs from the cupboard, she perused her tea selection.

"How about Strawberry Mango?"

"Sounds perfect."

Gina put bags in the teacups and said, "I haven't eaten lunch. I was going to nuke some Beecher's Macaroni and Cheese. Want some?"

"Maybe a little. I ate a late breakfast."

Gina got that going in the microwave and poured the boiling water into the mugs, smelling the tea begin to darken.

"How many paintings do you have left to do?" asked Melanie.

"Two to finish and two I haven't started yet."

"You know one of the climbing roses at the nursery, 'Madame Alfred Carriere', is going to open in the next couple of days."

"In April. Wow, that's early."

"It's on a stone wall fronted by gravel. It gets lots and lots of heat so it always blooms the earliest."

"That would be great. I'd love a rose in this group of paintings, but I thought it was too early for them to bloom."

"Not anymore. Global warming."

The buzzer on the microwave sounded and Gina stirred the still frozen food and put it back in.

She got out plates, forks and napkins. When the buzzer went off again, she dished up the macaroni and cheese. The rich cheddar smelled delicious.

They took their food to the table near the large windows overlooking Puget Sound and sat down.

"I needed comfort food," said Gina.

"Me too."

"Good, cause I also bought half a chocolate cake and I really shouldn't be eating it all."

They ate in silence for a few minutes. Gina savored the rich, sharp cheddar flavor.

Finally, Melanie said, "I've been feeling really uneasy ever since yesterday."

"What happened yesterday?"

"Mark Morris was at the nursery."

"I saw him, playing one-upmanship with Karl Erickman."

"Exactly. The two were walking around as if they owned the place."

"Do you think they're in the will?"

"I don't know if there was a will or not. None of us do. I hope that's solved soon. Karen talked to her brother, who's a lawyer. If there's no heir, the nursery will go to the state. Who will sell it to pay any debts. And guess who would be standing in line to buy it?"

"I don't think Karl Erickman wants it. He was just talking about buying specimen plants from the gardens. And Mark Morris' business is in England. I don't know if he can legally live here. What does it take for an Englishman to emigrate?"

"Money probably. And his family's rolling in it. Huge estate on massive acreage. Servants, the whole bit. His dad might be a duke or earl or something too. Money and aristocracy."

"So why would he want to buy Ravenswood?"

"He doesn't own any of his family's land. I remember Delia said once that his dad was young and Mark has lots of older siblings. He just gets some money every year. He won't get the estate. And what Delia's built here is amazing. She's got more fame than he does. You saw the last four days. People were devastated she's dead. She didn't have the money he does, though. He buys this place, he's got extra cachet. And taking over the nursery, to carry on her good work, just increases that tenfold."

"I don't see it, but I don't know the plant world like you do."

Gina sipped the hot tea, which tasted of summer. Strawberries. Her own would be ripening in close to a month.

Then it came to her and she set the mug down on the table.

She said, "They're in it together." Gina ran her hand through her hair. Why hadn't she seen it before?

"That would be crazy, but it does make a weird kind of sense," said Melanie.

"Wow. It does sound crazy. It's dependent on there being no will. And no family who could inherit the nursery. But who did the murdering and who stole the plants?"

"I don't know. Mark Morris is the stronger of the two. Karl Erickman is just so slimy."

"But venomous underneath, I suspect," said Gina.

"I wonder if Karen ever found time to check and see if other plants are missing."

"How could she have? She's been running like crazy for the last four days."

"But she's been closing," said Melanie.

"Last night she was going to water the tropical greenhouse after she closed. Plants were wilting in there, I told her about it."

"Karen could check on plants, water them and do three other things with her eyes closed and one hand tied behind her back."

"Yeah, she does seem to be pretty amazing," said Gina.

Gina picked up the dishes, got clean plates and silverware. She brought the cake over, along with a big knife.

"That's gorgeous," said Melanie.

"Isn't it? Couldn't resist."

Gina cut the cake and served up slices. Three layers with chocolate mousse in between each one and frosted with chocolate buttercream.

She took one bite and the deep, rich chocolate filled her mouth. The cake was moist and the frosting and mousse creamy. Decadence incarnate.

"Oh my," said Melanie.

"Yes."

After a time Gina said, "I don't know if he'll believe us."

"I don't know either. But we've got to try."

"Yes. We do," said Gina.

DAY 6 - WEDNESDAY

Gina made it to the nursery by nine the next morning. Which meant she had one week to get the paintings finished, framed, and the labels made. The day to hang everything was next Wednesday.

In the parking lot sat Melanie and Karen's pickups. Melanie had the shiny blue one and Karen, an old beat-up white one. Both were four-wheel drive, which was necessary to get around this area in the winter. Her Prius wasn't great in the ice and snow. She always just kept her supplies stocked up and stayed home during snowstorms. There were three other cars in the parking lot, ones she didn't recognize. She didn't know what everyone drove, but the cars told her that at least three other staff members were here.

She'd passed the Sheriff's and Deputies' vehicles parked in Delia and Renee's driveway. So they were working over there.

Walking past the tree peony which was blooming during the conference, she was disappointed to see it had dropped all its petals. There would be more flowers open soon, though. It was filled with buds. She didn't see anyone on her way to the tropical greenhouse and didn't seek them out.

Yesterday they'd probably watered everything and today they were most likely busy propagating plants. Their stock was really low. Brianna was probably back to work filling online, mail and phone orders. If she had the plants left to do that.

"Okay focus," Gina said to herself, setting up her paints in the tropical greenhouse. The gingers had opened up even more. She'd just have to paint around the changes.

She finished the red torch ginger first. It turned out quite well. She set the finished painting on top of some sturdy foliage to dry. That way a cat wouldn't come in and step on it. She'd learned the hard way to never set a painting on a flat surface.

The shell ginger was more complicated. Each bud along the drooping stalk was like painting a complete flower. She finished that up around noon. Then walked out into the cool fresh air, taking both the paintings out to her car to finish drying, and getting her lunch bag from the front seat.

Melanie and the others were sitting in the outside dining area. She joined them. Today Brianna, Tyler and Stacy were working. So David must be off.

"Well hello," said Stacy. "I didn't know you were here."

"I got here around nine. I've been hanging out in the tropical greenhouse. Finishing up yesterday's paintings."

"How do they look?" asked Melanie.

"I like them. They're not perfect, but then they never are."

"Sort of like gardening," said Karen. "There's always something left undone."

"Exactly," said Gina.

The conversation turned to upcoming events that they needed to prepare for. An open house was scheduled for mid June. They were going to have to work hard to keep the nursery and gardens looking nice. Even though the focus for the next month and a half was propagation.

Gina ate her smoked turkey and cheddar sandwich. The salad greens on it crunched nicely. The bread was whole grain and a little dry. She drank a lot of water in between bites. When she'd finished Gina felt satisfied.

Brianna said, "Well, I'd better get back to work before I fall asleep."

She got up and left, followed by Tyler and Stacy.

"Where is that rose you told me about?" she asked Melanie.

"Oh it's out at the edge of the sunny border. And you know that seep that runs through the woodland garden?"

"No. I didn't know there was a seep out there."

"Well, there is, you should really go check out the primroses. In the last couple of days all of them have exploded. It's truly a show."

"Okay, I'll go check things out."

"Have you seen the Sheriff today?" asked Melanie.

"No, you're the first people I've seen."

"I wonder how they're doing over there."

Meaning 'we should go talk to them about who the murderers are'.

"Don't know. Maybe we should go check, later in the afternoon."

"Sounds good. How about four? I'll be done then."

"I'll try to be finished. Depends on how fast things dry. And how long it takes me to find the next two things to paint."

"I'll come look for you if you don't show up."

"Okay," said Gina. She threw her trash away and went back to the greenhouse for her easel and paint bag.

She carried everything through the gardens. Then found the woodland area where the seep was. Along the meandering rivulets of water, a river of Primula had been planted. Candelabra primroses melded into double and common primroses in colors of light and dark purples, ranges of pink, pale oranges to bright oranges, yellows and even reds. The effect was glorious. A fairy land of color and texture.

She'd been by here giving tours a couple of days ago, but

nothing had been open. The sudden heat wave of the last couple of days had changed that.

There was one quite spectacular stalk that had blossoms of watermelon pink, edged with white and a yellow center. The unopened buds were red. It was quite the loveliest primrose she'd ever seen.

That was the one.

Gina set up her supplies and used some white oil pastel to outline the petals. Then she did a quick wash for the flower and the foliage. She lay it flat to dry a bit while she studied the flower. She took some photos just in case there was more work to do at home.

When the wash had dried enough, Gina began to lay in the watermelon color of the petals with her brush. Then the yellow center. She let that part alone and worked on the stalk and leaves.

Gina heard two men coming down the path, their shoes crunching the gravel. She recognized the voices. Karl Erickman and Mark Morris.

She took out her phone and called Melanie.

"Hi, do we have customers here today?"

"No. But Mark Morris and Karl Erickman are walking about. Said they were having a horticultural disagreement and wanted to check something out. Stacy told them it was okay."

"Okay. I'd feel better if someone was out here with me though."

"Ooh, it's break time for me, then. Where are you?"

"Primroses."

"Okay, I'll be there shortly."

"Thanks," said Gina.

She felt slightly foolish. But they had probably murdered two people. She didn't want to be number three. If they were the murderers they were either incredibly stupid or incredibly brazen.

She couldn't decide which.

They were walking down the path, talking and oblivious to her presence.

She kept painting, laying down the intense color of the primrose.

"I've always just hated that plant," said Karl.

"What is it that you've got against Rhodies?" asked Mark.

"They're such a cliche in gardens around here."

"They aren't overused in this garden. And you know they're not a cliche in England. We struggle to make our soil more acidic, so they'll survive."

"Well, I hate them," said Karl

"Maybe someday you and I will own this garden and we can change it however we want."

"I can hardly wait."

"But we have to find that Vietnamese plant," said Mark. "I don't know if the cuttings have taken yet, wasn't able to get into those greenhouses, too many people around. The drug company that Delia contracted with will want them, and soon. That's when we'll get the money."

"We'll find it. Does it really have to be exclusive? Are you sure we can't sell it to another company too? Under a slightly different name?"

"Yes, I'm sure. Their money plus mine will be enough. Let's not pile on the illegalities."

They stopped talking. Gina decided they must have spotted her.

"Oh hello," said Karl Erickman. "The artist at work."

Gina glanced up and then looked back at her work, not missing a brush stroke.

"Oh hi. Didn't hear you coming. I've got to get those paintings done for the gallery opening."

"You didn't hear us coming?" asked Mark, a suspicious look on his face. "We were making a lot of noise."

They had stopped close enough to touch her. Their presence

made her nervous. She took a breath, concentrating on her painting. She didn't want to betray her nervousness.

"My hearing just isn't what it used to be. Getting old and I went to far too many concerts in my younger days."

"That does destroy one's hearing," Karl said.

Gina didn't looked at either of them to see if they believed her or not. She pretended to be completely focused on her work. Layering in the details.

"That's such a beautiful Primula," said Mark.

"It is, isn't it. I don't know if I've seen another to match it," she said.

"I meant the painting," he said.

"Oh, thank you."

"The flower is stunning, but you've deepened the colors and brought out some detail that most people would have missed. Quite a wonderful painting," said Mark.

"Well thank you. It helps to have such a nice subject."

About then, she heard more gravel crunching. Melanie. Gina didn't look up, pretending she didn't hear her, but kept on painting.

"Oh, everyone's come out to see the Primulas," Melanie said. "I was so sad they weren't open for the conference folks. It's always such a magical time of year around here when the primroses bloom."

"Aren't they just charming," said Mark.

"I do like the cowslips," said Karl.

"That's because you're not from England," said Mark. "They're all over the place where I live."

It was obviously a reference to their previous conversation.

Gina didn't pay any attention to it.

"Oh, that's lovely, Gina," said Melanie. "I brought you a soda, thought you must be thirsty with all this heat."

"Thank you," Gina said, taking the can of soda. "It's almost done. Perhaps I can finish my paintings today, after all."

"That would be a relief."

"Yes, it would. I'm really behind. With working here unexpectedly for the conference and recovering from it, I lost five days of work. Usually, I've got all the paintings framed and ready to go a week or two ahead of time. I'm cutting it close this time."

"It'll be fine," said Melanie.

"I'm sure it will. I've just been a little panicked, that's all."

"Well, we should go check out that Arisaema," said Karl.

"Yes, we should," replied Mark.

"See you later," said Melanie.

"Bye," said Gina.

Karl Erickman glanced back suspiciously at her as the path rounded a bend. The look sent shivers up Gina's spine.

When they were out of earshot, Gina said, "Thanks for coming out. I'm such a coward."

"No, you're smart. Two murders in less than a week. And we're not really sure why."

Gina told her about the men's conversation she'd just overheard.

"Okay, we really do need to go talk to the Sheriff. Now."

"I agree. I want out of the garden as long as those two are around."

"You're right. We can walk past the rose on the way to the house. You can snap a couple of photos to paint from."

"Thanks."

"I don't like the idea of any of us being way out here alone. Before all this I had no problems with it. But until the murderers are caught, it's just not safe. I'm going to have a talk with the others about it."

"I think you should."

Gina handed the painting to Melanie to carry. Then she picked up the easel and her supply bag. They walked quickly through the woodland garden to the sunny border. Gina set her things down and took three photos of the rose with her phone.

"Let's go," Gina whispered, picking up her things. "We should be careful what we talk about, they might hear."

Melanie nodded.

They moved quickly towards the nursery.

"Oh, I do love that rose. I might have to buy that painting myself," said Melanie

"I'd happily give it to you," Gina said.

"But then you'd have to paint another painting for the show. Nope. I'm a working woman. I've got money. Just tell the gallery they can mark that one as sold."

"You might not like the frame I put on it."

"I'm not buying it for the frame, silly."

They didn't meet the two men again, which was just fine with her.

"I need to put these in the car."

"Great, I'll come with you."

In the parking lot there were only three vehicles left. Gina's, Melanie's and Karen's. Gina sighed a deep breath of relief. She'd been a little afraid Mark and Karl might be out here, waiting for them.

She put her things in the car, spreading it out to fully dry. Melanie was on the phone to Karen, warning her.

Gina locked the car and they headed towards the office. Once past it, they took the narrow gravel path through the gate and over to the house.

The path wove through tall native shrubs and trees. Thimbleberry, flowering currant with its drooping pink racemes, salmonberry, Indian plum with its fading white blooms, second growth cedars, tall firs, stately big leaf maples with drooping yellow clusters of flowers and diminutive vine maples. Sprinkled throughout were both evergreen and deciduous huckleberries bushes. Thorny-leafed Mahonia with their yellow flowers just beginning to fade. Covering the ground lay salal, sword ferns and Oxalis oregana. The forest felt cool and secluded. The raucous calls of blue jays and gravel crunching beneath their feet were the only sounds. Somewhere high overhead, Gina heard an eagle calling.

The path hadn't been trimmed lately and Gina, who was leading the way, kept getting slapped in the face by branches. Delia had obviously liked the area around the house kept wild. Possibly to discourage visitors from the nursery.

The log house came into view not long before the back patio appeared. The area lay covered with large yellowish-gray paving stones interspersed with a moss. A forest green metal table, umbrella and four all weather chairs sat waiting for people who would never sit there again.

They walked around the side of the house on a path set with the same paving stones. A window on the side of the house was lit up inside with grow lights. Succulents filled the windowsill.

At the front door they knocked.

A Deputy Gina had seen before, answered. She was medium height with an angular face and short, curly brown hair. Her nameplate said Deputy Corinne Hammond.

"Is the Sheriff here?"

"Yes, come in," the young woman said.

They went inside. The house smelled closed up and stuffy.

"Sheriff Jansson," said the Deputy, loudly.

There were piles of papers sitting on the couch, on the chairs, separate piles on the dining room table. On every flat surface.

The Sheriff poked his head out from the kitchen area. He looked tired and disheveled.

"Hello ladies, I'm in here."

They went into the kitchen and found it looked the same. Stacks of paper on every counter and the kitchen table. Only the sink, stove and the island in the center of the room were clear.

"Where did all the papers come from?" asked Melanie. "This house is always so clean and uncluttered."

"Each of the offices has rows of file cabinets. Plus there's an attic, filled with boxes."

"What is it?" asked Gina.

He said, "A mixture of things, business records, personal records. And it looks like information from every class that Delia taught."

"Wow," said Gina. "I probably have that much paper, too. Guess I should go through a lot of it and toss it. We only moved out here three years ago, but stuff accumulates so quickly. And there's so much of Ewan's papers that I didn't get rid of when he died."

"I've lived in my house for over thirty years. I'm not even going to think about it. If my kids want the house, they're going to have to work for it," said Melanie.

Gina laughed.

"So, what can I do for you?" asked the Sheriff, sipping on a bottle of iced tea.

Gina hesitated and said, "Well, it might be something silly, but I think we figured out who murdered Delia and Renee, or we could be completely wrong."

"Have a seat," he said, pointing to the kitchen island.

They pulled up the tall chairs with leather backs on them, and sat.

He asked, "Water?" He pointed to the bottled water sitting next to an opened box of chocolate cookies on the marble counter. "And we've got cookies. Help yourself."

Melanie shook her head. Gina took a bottle, opened it and drank, swallowing a couple sips of the room temperature water. She hadn't realized how thirsty she was.

Gina asked, "Have you learned anything about the drug companies?"

The Sheriff said, "It looks like that's a dead end. Mostly. Delia did contact them, but they all declined her offer to view the plant. Except one company, who did send someone out. After the visit, they said they weren't interested. Nearly all the companies said their research and development budgets had been cut or that they were full up for pursuing new drug sources."

"That's weird," said Melanie. "They're making so much money from new drugs, how can they turn down possible new sources?"

"I thought it was strange too, but I asked around and apparently most of the companies do go through phases where they are using all their people to work on what they've already obtained, testing those products and they really can't take anything else on. Not without hiring more people and finding more lab space. Which is a considerable expense, for a long shot," he said.

"So, you've decided it couldn't have been them?" asked Gina. "I overheard Mark Morrison this afternoon say that Delia had it all set up with a drug company."

"This afternoon?" asked the Sheriff.

"He and Karl Erickman were touring the gardens this afternoon," said Melanie.

"What did he say exactly?" asked the Sheriff.

"Something about the drug company Delia contracted with. That they'd want the plants soon. He and Karl were talking about owning the nursery. And that Mark hadn't found the Vietnamese plant yet. He hadn't been able to search the greenhouses because there were too many people around."

"So you think, it was Mark Morrison and Karl Erickman? Why?" he asked.

"They've both been at the nursery every day, including today," Gina said.

He raised his eyebrows.

"Wait, I thought the nursery was closed today," he said.

"They came and walked through the gardens. They told Stacy they wanted to look at a plant in the garden to settle a plant identification dispute," said Melanie.

"Hm. Go on."

Gina told him about the other conversations between them that she'd overheard and about Karl's interest in what would happen to the nursery.

"I think they intend to buy the nursery from either the heir or the state. I doubt if they're in the will. If there is a will," said Melanie.

"And that would be worth murdering for?" asked the Sheriff.

"Not for most people," said Melanie. "but they have connections, knowledge and money. I think they intend to build on Delia's work. Mark had intended to buy in with Delia and Renee. Maybe Delia told him Renee wouldn't have it. Or maybe he's just taking any deal he can get."

The Sheriff leaned back in his chair.

"I came to the same conclusion myself this morning. However, at this point, I have no real proof. We obviously still haven't found a will. We've contacted all the estate attorneys in the area and none of them have any record of one. We're looking for other legal papers, thinking perhaps Delia and Renee went to a firm in Seattle. We've seen no evidence that either Delia or Renee had any contact with family members, and we've found no next of kin for either of them. It's as if they sprang out of nowhere. It's early still, but unless someone comes forward soon, it looks like the property will go to the state."

"So basically, you need either a will with Mark or Karl's name on it, and/or proof that the two of them committed the murder," said Gina. She picked up one of the crunchy chocolate cookies and was surprised by a soft peanut butter center. She was hungry. It was time for dinner.

"The will, if one of them is the heir, won't be enough. We need good solid proof," the Sheriff said.

"Could you get a warrant to search for the missing plants?" asked Melanie.

"We haven't got enough evidence to take that step yet."

"What do you need?" Melanie asked.

"DNA would be good."

"That's your department," said Gina. "If there was any to get, wouldn't you have found it already?"

"Not necessarily. Not if they went somewhere on the property other than where we've collected DNA."

"Well, they've been there for five days now. They could have left plenty of it behind. How would you even be able to tell what's from the murders and what's not?" asked Gina.

"Location."

Just then a whooping sound came in from another room.

The Sheriff stood.

Deputy Hofsteader came walking in, a huge grin on his face. He was waving an emerald green file folder.

"Will," he said.

He handed it to the Sheriff.

Gina's heart was pounding.

She hoped it would tell them something about a possible murderer.

The Sheriff sat down again and opened the file folder and began reading the papers. It took several pages before he looked up and said, "With both Delia and Renee dead, Karen inherits the nursery. And the house."

"Karen will be so happy. She works so hard," said Melanie.

"But does that mean that Karen murdered them?" asked Gina.

"It's possible she doesn't even know," said the Sheriff. "They may not have told her. Most people don't expect to die in the near future, let alone so young."

He flipped through the papers and said, "It's dated two years ago."

"Where's the law firm located?" asked Gina.

He looked and said, "Seattle. And the executor's name is Suzanne Majors. Does that name ring a bell?"

Gina shook her head.

"No," said Melanie.

"Well, she may be a friend or she may have been hired by the estate and working for a fee. I'd have to wade through all this to see if it says."

"So, this doesn't really tell you anything?" said Gina.

"Not clearly. But the next step is to talk to Karen. I want your promise not to breathe a word of this to anyone until I talk to her."

"I won't," said Gina. "It's your news to give to her."

"I won't either," said Melanie.

They left the house. The parking lot was empty when they got there.

Which was a relief. Gina had been half afraid that the two men might have come back. She didn't want to see either Mark Morrison and Karl Erickman ever again. Not until she was sure they weren't murderers.

Gina felt excited about Karen inheriting. She couldn't see it in Karen to be a murderer. The woman was strong, but she was far too kind to kill for an inheritance.

The two men, however, they frightened her to the bone.

DAY 7 - THURSDAY

The next morning Gina was drinking tea and staring at her collection of empty picture frames. Trying to match them up with the paintings. It was no good, she was going to have to find a couple more of the ornate fussy ones. Many of the ones she had were simply the wrong sizes.

Less than a week till hanging for the show.

Well, she could do that tomorrow. Make a run through town and hit the secondhand and antique shops. And if she didn't find what she wanted, there was Stanwood. And Marysville. And Everett and Snohomish. One way or another, she'd find the frames she needed.

The wind and rain had been pounding down on her little house since the middle of the night. The upper thirds of the cedars were bent over in the wind.

Then her power went out.

She went around the house unplugging things and turning them off. Even things plugged into surge protectors. She'd lost a TV a couple years back, even though it was plugged through a surge protector. The power coming back on had zapped it anyway.

After half an hour, Gina decided it was time to light a fire. She opened up the wood stove and put in newspaper, kindling and one stick of firewood, then lit it. It took about five minutes and more firewood and she had a blazing fire.

Her cell phone rang and she picked it up.

"Gina, good, you're home. I'm bringing Karen over." It was Melanie.

"Why?"

"I'll tell you when we get there. Put on the teakettle." Melanie's voice sounded pinched and upset.

"Okay," said Gina.

Melanie hung up.

Gina put a kettle of water on the wood stove, then tidied up the living room and kitchen.

She unlocked the front door and was just getting out mugs and put shortbread cookies on a plate, when the cats scattered, their claws making scuffling noises on the floor. Melanie and Karen came bursting through the door.

"Hi," said Melanie. "Sorry for such short notice. Karen was attacked."

"Did you call the Sheriff?" asked Gina, her heart pounding.

"Yes, he told us to lock ourselves in the office. Then when he got there, he told us to leave. Police cars were flooding in. After he talked to Karen, he told us to go somewhere nearby, with a Deputy and wait. We came here since it was close."

"Does the Deputy want to come in?"

"No, he wanted to be outside, standing guard."

"Well, come in and take your coats off, you're drenched," said Gina.

"It's an awful storm," said Melanie. "There's no power at the nursery. Oh, you don't have power either. Stupid me."

"The wood stove's going, the water's heating. We'll be fine."

She ushered them into the living room. Karen stood by the wood stove. Her face looking worried. No frightened.

The water in the kettle was steaming.

"What type of tea do you want? I've got black, green, herbal."

"Black," said Melanie.

"Black," repeated Karen.

"Black it is," said Gina.

She got out a teapot and poured some loose tea with orange peel, roses and bergamot flowers in it. Then poured in the hot water. Closed the lid and put a tea cosy over the pot.

"Are you two cold?" asked Gina, putting more wood on the fire.

"A little," said Karen.

"Yes," said Melanie. "We were stuck in the office for a couple of hours and there was no power or heat. We'd left our coats in the greenhouses where we were working."

Gina got a soft throw out of the closet and wrapped it around Karen's shoulders. She pulled another one out for Melanie.

"The tea will be ready in a couple of minutes. Do you want to sit down?"

Karen looked numb. She finally nodded and walked over to the couch and sat down. Gina got her another throw for her legs. Karen pulled it up around her as if for protection.

Melanie sat on the other end of the couch.

Albert came walking out of the bedroom, jumped up on the couch and sat in Karen's lap. She petted him as if she wasn't even thinking about it. His big purr filled the emptiness.

Gina poured the tea and asked, "Cream anyone?"

"Yes," they both said.

She got the cream out and splashed it in cups and returned it to the fridge, hastily closing the door. She hoped the power wouldn't be out too long. She'd just bought groceries.

Gina carried the mugs out, handing one to Melanie and setting Karen's on the side table next to her. She added more wood to the fire and then got her own mug and the cookies. She put the cookies on the coffee table within reach of everyone and sat down in a chair.

Then there was a knock on the door.

Karen and Melanie both jumped, but Albert stayed put.

Gina got up and went to the door. She looked through the peephole and saw the Sheriff. He waved at her.

She opened the door and said, "Come in."

"Thank you. How are they?"

"Melanie's jumpy and Karen's in shock."

"Nasty business."

"Would you like some tea?"

"Thank you. I'd love some," he said.

"You can hang your coat there," she said, pointing to the hooks in the entryway.

He took off his raincoat and she went to pour another mug of tea.

"Cream?" she asked.

"Real cream?" He raised his eyebrows.

She nodded.

"Oh yes."

After she poured in a large splash of cream, he took the mug from her and sat down in a chair.

"It's nice and warm in here," he said.

"Yes, I'd just started a fire, when Melanie called."

He turned to Karen and Melanie. "Well, ladies. I'm sorry to have to take you through all this again, but I really do need to hear what happened another time. Can you do that?"

"I can," said Karen. "But I'm worried about my dogs. What if the attackers went to my house, to wait for me."

"I've already sent a Deputy over to your house, just to make sure they're not there. You told me the dogs are outside in the fenced yard. He'll make sure they're safe. He's good with dogs. And Max will recognize him."

Karen looked visibly relieved.

She began talking.

"I was in the mist greenhouse. Checking on the cuttings we have in there. Making sure they'd gotten enough water and not too much. Too much and they'll rot. Some of them are beginning to leaf out. I finished up and walked outside. Someone grabbed me from behind and began choking me. I kicked and elbowed. And screamed. I must have gotten him hard enough to cause some pain."

She sipped her tea, then continued.

"He loosened his grip and that was when Melanie came running from another greenhouse with a hoe. Screaming."

At that Karen grinned.

"If it wasn't so awful, I'd laugh. It was such a funny sight. He let go and took off. I ran the opposite direction, towards Melanie."

Melanie said, "He kept on going, off through the woods. Karen and I ran to the office and locked ourselves in and called you. Neither of us were sure if there might actually be two of them, one hiding in the bushes somewhere. And the office wasn't heated because the power had gone out and no one was in there today, anyway. We didn't even know it was out, because neither of us had been using anything that needed power."

"Did you see his face?" asked the Sheriff.

"Ski mask," Melanie said.

"His breath smelled of coffee," said Karen. "Not much to go on."

"He was a bit taller than Karen, maybe six inches. And he had on jeans, a black jacket and a black ski mask," said Melanie.

"And black Nikes. I remember, cause I was trying to stomp on his foot with my work boots."

"They're still searching the nursery and the surrounding area. I think they were after you, Karen. Is there anyplace you can go, off the island for a few days. Someplace where no one will find you?"

"My brother lives in Bellingham. I could go stay with him. He works at home and he has a dog too, so I could bring Jack and Max."

"Good. When you're ready, I'll have the Deputy drive you back to your house so you can get what you need and then he'll drive you and the dogs, to Bellingham. We'll find someone to stay there with you."

"Is this attack because I inherited the nursery?"

"That's my guess."

"Am I always going to have to be looking over my shoulder all the time? Worried about being murdered? If so, then the nursery's not worth it."

"Not if we catch the people behind Delia and Renee's deaths. Which we're working really hard to do. After I talked to you last night, did you tell anyone about your inheritance?"

"I did. I emailed the entire nursery staff. I thought they'd want to know their jobs were still there."

"And word spread from there?" asked the Sheriff.

"Apparently," said Melanie.

Karen sipped her tea, petting Albert who was still purring.

Gina took a cookie and bit into it. The buttery flavor felt comforting.

The Sheriff continued to ask Karen questions about details she couldn't answer. The color of the man's eyes, was any hair visible through the holes of the ski mask? Any rings?

Karen opened the blanket a bit to reveal the bruise around her neck. It wasn't as bad as many Gina had seen on TV shows when someone was choked, even though those had all been makeup. Presumably, they were based on reality.

"How does your throat feel?" asked the Sheriff.

"Okay. Sore, but okay."

"And did you black out at any point?"

"No. I was just so afraid. Even more when I was running away."

"I think you'll be fine. If you develop any problems, get to a doctor, okay?"

"I will."

They finished their tea.

Karen said, "I want to get going. I need to call my brother and get the dogs."

"Why don't you call now," said the Sheriff.

Melanie went out to the entryway and got Karen's purse.

Gina added more wood to the fire and asked, "Who wants more tea?"

"Me," said Melanie.

"I'll have another cup," said the Sheriff.

She poured another round.

Karen got hold of her brother and then left with the Deputy.

The Sheriff saw her to the door and then came back and sat down.

Albert curled up on the throw, unperturbed at losing his lap.

"Wow," said Gina. "I didn't expect that."

"Neither did I and I should have. They've already killed twice," said the Sheriff.

"But how did they know about the will being found unless they had friends in the nursery?" asked Melanie.

"They had a friend in the nursery," said Gina. "David."

Melanie looked at her.

"Has David ever worn black Nikes or a black jacket?" asked the Sheriff.

"I don't know," said Melanie.

"Was he scheduled to work today?"

"No, Karen said he took a few days off to go camping."

"I already sent a Deputy to his house. I guess we'll see if he's off camping," said the Sheriff.

"Are the rest of us safe being at the nursery?" asked Melanie.

"I don't know. I'll be keeping a Deputy there until we catch the killers."

"Good, cause there's plants that need watering. Things that need tending to, or we'll lose the whole year's worth of plants to sell. And Brianna has orders to get out."

"Can you work in groups?"

"I guess we'll have to, won't we?" said Melanie.

Gina sipped her tea, rolling the creamy warm liquid around in her mouth.

"Thanks Gina, for being available," said Melanie.

"I'm glad I could help."

The Sheriff's phone rang and he answered.

Gina got up and stirred the fire a bit, then added more wood.

When the Sheriff had finished his phone call, he said, "David's supposedly at work. That's what his mother said."

"He lives with his mother?" asked Gina.

"Yeah," said Melanie. "I vaguely remember that. Twenty-two years old and still living with his mom. It's hard for kids these days. Working part time in a nursery isn't a money making proposition. Neither is working full time in a nursery. I couldn't do it if the house wasn't paid off."

"So, what would he be getting out of this deal?" asked the Sheriff. "Money? Career Advancement?"

"I don't know," said Melanie. "I've never really talked to him. I don't even know if this job was just a job or his real work."

Gina said, "He might have been promised money. I don't know if either Karl Erickman or Mark Morris would want to live out here in the sticks and manage the nursery on a day to day basis. They might, but Mark has a nursery in England and Karl has one in Seattle. They can't be everywhere."

"But David doesn't know enough to manage. He's young and immature. And his plant knowledge doesn't run that deep. Not at that age. It might if he was passionate about plants, but he's not," said Melanie.

The Sheriff said, "He might not be a good manager, but they still might have him tagged to manage, with them overseeing. Or they might be planning to get rid of him when it's convenient. We don't know who actually murdered Delia or Renee. It might have been David, or it might have been one of the others or both."

"So, really, there's no proof of anything yet," said Gina.

"We have a description of the shoes. And fresh tracks running off into the woods, we can get a shoe size. We have a vague description. We have a few other hints. A picture is beginning to form of what happened over the last week. We've got a few more things we're investigating and waiting for information to come in on. I think this will all come together just fine," said the Sheriff.

Gina wasn't so sure and she could tell Melanie wasn't either.

The Sheriff's phone rang again.

"No." He paused. Then said, "Keep them there. I'd like to talk to them." Clicking his phone off, he said, "Well, thank you for your hospitality. The tea was much needed. I've got to get back to work."

"Haven't you been working while you've been here?" asked Gina.

"Yes, but it's been warm and dry. Now, I get to go back out into the rain and work," he grinned. "I don't have enough deputies to leave any with the two of you. I don't think you're at risk, you're not on the will, but promise me you'll keep your doors locked, at home and while driving. If you see or hear anything suspicious, please call immediately."

"I'll do that," said Melanie. "Can I work in the nursery tomorrow?"

"Yes. Who else is scheduled?"

"Brianna, Tyler and Stacy. And of course Karen."

"I'll keep a lookout for you," he said.

Gina felt safe enough in her own home.

The Sheriff got his coat and left. Gina put more water to boil on the wood stove.

"You're welcome to stay," said Gina. "It's warm here, your place won't be."

"I might have power at my house," she said.

"True."

"I'll call my neighbor and find out."

Melanie called.

Gina stirred the fire and made another pot of tea. Just in case.

Melanie clicked off her phone after a short conversation.

"Power's out."

"Sorry. Soup for lunch?"

"That works for me. I've got a cold sandwich in the truck. What can I do to help?"

"Nothing, I made the soup for dinner the other night. Just need to reheat it."

"You cooked?"

"I did. Amazing, huh?"

Gina took a container from the fridge and poured it into a saucepan. Then she set the pan on the wood stove.

There was a loud cracking sound outside followed by a crash and the ground shook.

They both looked at each other and Gina went to the front door, opening it and walking outside in the wind.

Stretching across the road lay a twenty-five foot long chunk of a Douglas fir. Beneath part of it sat a neighbor's caved-in car. On Gina's side of the street, the bottom three-fourths of the now topless tree stood, in a different neighbor's yard.

"Wow," said Melanie. "It just missed my truck."

"Maybe you should move your truck into the carport."

"What are the odds?" asked Melanie.

Gina just stared at her.

"You're right. After two murders and an attack, odds aren't looking too good."

Melanie got in her car and parked it next to Gina's.

Other neighbors were coming out of their houses to move their cars and assess the damage. Two of them went into their garages and got out chainsaws. Staying well away from the downed power line.

"Crazy people," said Melanie.

"Yup. Hope the power doesn't come back on."

They stood beneath Gina's eaves, on the porch and out of the rain and watched the neighbors working together to cut up the tree and drag the pieces off, so the road was clear. The compact car was totaled, though.

A few minutes later, a Snohomish County Public Utility District truck pulled up and a guy got out, waving people off. He talked to the two chainsaw wielding men and they nodded. Then another larger truck rolled up, one with a basket. It went to a pole and a worker got in the basket and raised it to the top of one pole and then the other. After a few minutes he'd cut the cables that had been partially broken.

Once those fell to the ground, the chain saw men began again. The first man from the PUD truck pulled a chainsaw from his truck and helped them.

Gina said, "Wow, that basket is really swaying."

And it was. The worker was able to get it back down. Brave person.

The wind continued to gust. They finally got the road cleared.

There were plenty of smaller branches blowing past. The trees had just begun to leaf out and the leaves were catching the wind. Usually the hard storms came in winter. Not this time. Nature was pruning.

"I better go check the soup," said Gina.

She went back in and stirred the boiling soup.

They got out bowls and Melanie helped her set the table. They had lunch looking out at the Sound. It was a bit nerve wracking when stray branches hit the windows.

The sausage in the vegetable soup was just spicy enough to give it some zing, but not enough to be too hot.

"This soup is great," said Melanie. "It's calming. Just what I needed. I was so afraid all morning."

"What an awful thing to happen," said Gina.

"Poor Karen," said Melanie.

"Did you lock the door?" asked Gina.

"Yes. I don't want to see any of those three again."

"Me neither. Do you think the nursery will be okay in the storm?"

"Who knows. Delia kept trees trimmed, but there's always some storm damage. I'll find out tomorrow," said Melanie

"I wouldn't want to be working there, hunting for suspects, in this windstorm."

"Me neither."

"What do you think the Sheriff meant when he said waiting for information to come in?" Gina asked.

"I don't know."

"Maybe phone records. Or bank account information. Or travel records," said Gina

"Or seized computers with email records and business records? From Karl and Mark?"

"They wouldn't have been stupid enough to leave that kind of trail, would they?"

"We can hope they were," said Melanie.

After lunch, Melanie helped Gina mat and frame some of the paintings. When they finished five paintings were lined up on a shelf, ready to go, despite Alice's attempts to help.

"They look beautiful. I can hardly wait for your opening, I'm so excited."

"They look good. Halfway there."

She still had two paintings to frame, that she already had frames for. And three paintings that she needed to find frames for. Gina took photos of those paintings on her phone. It might help when she was shopping for them tomorrow.

Melanie got a call from her neighbor when their power came back on.

"You want to come over to my house?" she asked.

"No, I'm good here. I've got the wood stove, candles, food and water."

"Okay, but call if you change your mind."

"I'll do that. Stay safe."

"You too."

Gina locked the door after Melanie left and put more firewood in the wood stove. After a dinner of the rest of the soup, she curled up on the couch with the cats, a battery powered lantern and more Janet Evanovich.

Somehow reading about murders made the actuality of the recent murders fade a bit. It didn't lessen her grief, though.

DAY 8 - FRIDAY

Gina was sitting in her car just outside the fourth antique store of the day when her cell phone rang.

"Hello."

"Gina, it's me, Melanie. What a morning."

"Everything okay?"

"No, but nothing you can do about it."

"Okay, what?"

"Several of Delia's trees came down. The mist greenhouse has a big one lying across it. That tree took down several others. They're cutting them apart now, so we'll see how much we've lost when they finish."

"Wow."

"And that's not the half of it. There's tons of sheriffs and deputies here again today. From all over. They're still looking for evidence. And one of the deputies who I know, from Raven Island, told me that Delia and Renee's house was broken into last night."

"Really? Was anything taken?"

"They're trying to figure that out. I guess they'd put most of the papers back where they found them. They took the rest as evidence. So there wasn't anything left that they needed."

"That they know of."

"Yeah."

"How are Maisie and Flopsy?"

"Freaked out. I just finished lunch and I'm at the pet store, buying two carriers for them. I'm bringing them home with me tonight. The plastic on the tropical greenhouse is shredded. So there aren't any heated greenhouses any more. And there's not anyone really there, not with Karen gone."

"Will the tropical plants be okay?"

"We'll find out. Summer's coming. Although we may be having a tropical plant sale of the specimen plants. We don't propagate them, or even sell them. Delia and Renee just liked them. But we don't need to be spending money on electricity to keep them happy all winter. That would be my take on it."

"Any word on Karen?" asked Gina.

"The Sheriff told me that she arrived safely and is driving the Deputy crazy by pacing. She wants to be back at work."

"Can't blame her. She just got handed this lovely gift and she can't even appreciate it."

"She'll get the chance. I'm sure of it. They'll catch the bad guys."

"I sure hope so," said Gina. "And soon."

"Yeah. Hey, how's your frame hunting going?"

"I found two that are perfect, need one more. I'm over in Marysville just about to go into a store."

"If you find it today and you have some extra time, we could use an extra hand here tomorrow. No guilt if you can't though."

"You must be really short handed."

"Yes. We could have used everyone today. Tyler and Stacy are trying to put up new plastic on the tropical greenhouse. You can imagine how well that's going."

Gina laughed. The two of them were very, very young. And unfocused.

"Exactly," said Melanie. "Brianna's filling orders as fast as she can, trying to get plants out of the nursery. I'm doing everything else. So, no Karen, no David, no Delia. I'm probably going to have to hire someone. Won't that be fun? Oh, and we've got a couple of groups coming tomorrow. I didn't think they could get hold of everyone to cancel on such short notice, so I confirmed they could come."

"Yes, I'll come in tomorrow. I'll have four days to get those last five paintings framed. I'll be able to do it."

"Well, dress for mud. It'll be a mess moving all those plants out of the trashed greenhouse. In between the two groups. Oh, and I'll need to give a tour to each of the groups."

"This is a train-wreck isn't it?" asked Gina.

"You said it."

"Okay, I'd better get moving then."

"Thanks so much. I owe you one. See you tomorrow," said Melanie.

Gina sat in her car staring blankly at the store in front of her.

Why would someone break into Delia and Renee's house now? After the police had been through it so thoroughly? What on earth were they looking for?

She got out of her car and shut the door, locking it. The sunny day had turned out very pleasant. T-shirt, jeans and running shoes weather. The windstorm yesterday must have gotten all the rain out of its system.

Gina went into the antique mall. Each section had things on consignment from a different vendor. She never knew what she'd find here. She was looking for a frame painted gold or bronze. Something sufficiently ornate to match that fluffy coral peony painting. Or one she could spray paint gold.

The place smelled pleasantly of old wood and felt like soft, well-used fabrics. Everything in here had a history. Glittery mirror balls from another age hung from the ceiling. Soft big band music played over the sound system. At the cash register stood a bowl of wrapped candies for customers. She took a peppermint and unwrapped it, to freshen up her mouth. The flavor was soft and subtle for a peppermint. Just as she liked them.

She walked through rows of oak furniture, then another section with dishes, clothes and knick knacks, all from the fifties. Things she recognized from her childhood.

The next part had kitchen tools. Pans, bowls, egg beaters and rolling pins, all made before she was even born.

Antique shops always intrigued her. Who had owned these things? What had their lives been like? Had they loved that vase? Or was it a gift from an in-law who was always critical and it brought back bad memories, so they got rid of it? Vintage stores were full of stories, if one knew how to ask and listen.

Then another section filled with Christmas decorations spanning a variety of decades. Another part contained an entire bedroom, minus the bed. Chenille bedspreads and hanging curtains. A nightstand topped with an exotic lamp and a stack of antique hardback books.

The next grouping was for living room items. Side tables with ancient lamps, some even with ragged silk covering the wiring. There were several framed paintings. None of the frames were right though.

Then in the next section she found the perfect frame. Painted gold, it had flowers carved in the wood. Some of them were even peonies. And there were fleur de lis, fronds and swirls. The frame was garishly ornate. Perfect.

Gina pulled a small tape measure out of her purse and measured it. It was a bit large, but she could compensate for that with the mat. It was awfully gold. She might mist it with a darker color of spray paint or rub some acrylic paint, just to take some of the gloss off and give the details some shadow. She'd have to get it home and see before deciding.

She glanced at the price and blanched. Thirty-five dollars was quite a bit for a frame. Maybe she could talk them down. Otherwise, she'd have to raise the price for the painting higher than the others.

She went to the cash register and said, "Is this frame really thirty-five? Seems like a lot for an empty frame."

The young woman looked at the price tag and said, "This is for the painting and the frame."

"There was no painting, I found this on the floor, leaning up against an old trunk."

"Just a minute. Marjorie!" the woman called.

An older woman emerged from the back. She looked frazzled, her hair sticking up all over and her apron smudged with dirt.

"Yes?"

"This frame's priced to go with a painting, but there was no painting. It was sitting on the floor."

"Oh, I remember. The other day a woman bought the painting, she didn't want the frame, too fussy, she said. I forgot to reprice the frame."

"So how much is it?" asked Gina.

"Five bucks, plus tax. Ornate frames just aren't very popular these days."

"Sold," Gina said. "It's perfect for what I need it."

"What are you going to do with it?" asked the older woman, ringing her up and taking her cash.

"I have a painting that really needs something this ornate."

"Well, I'm glad it's going to a good home."

"Thanks," said Gina, taking the receipt and the frame.

She got in the car and stood the frame in front of the others on the passenger seat floor.

Mission accomplished.

After a quick late lunch, or was it an early dinner, at a fast food burger place, she headed home, in rush hour traffic on the freeway. Friday afternoons the rush began at two and lasted well past six. The worst traffic of the week.

It was after six when she finally made it home. The cats were complaining. She stowed the frames in her studio and closed the door again. Cats were never allowed unchaperoned in the studio. Otherwise she'd have to pick all her work and supplies up every time.

She fed the cats. Then showered and got into pajamas. She checked her messages and email, nothing from Joanna yet. Then glanced at the weather report. Tomorrow was supposed to be even warmer and still sunny.

She set out jeans, a t-shirt, and some grubby older running shoes. And the clean Ravenswood Nursery hoodie. She'd bring her rubber boots along too. And a raincoat. Just in case. She made a tuna sandwich, then packed some carrot sticks, cookies and yogurt. And set a water bottle on the counter.

By the time she finished, it was nearly bedtime.

It had been a long day.

She lay in bed, just before dozing off.

What stories did the things in Delia and Renee's house have to tell? Who had broken into their house and what had they looked at? What were they searching for? Had they taken something?

The things that had been important to the two women were plants and art. Delia had some houseplants at the house? Had one of those been valuable?

She should ask Melanie.

Tomorrow.

DAY 9 - SATURDAY

Gina got to the nursery at a quarter to nine. She left her boots, raincoat and lunch in the car. Bringing only her cell phone and water bottle. She zipped the car keys into a pocket of the hoodie.

The parking lot was half-filled with various law enforcement vehicles. Not great for customers, but then again, maybe it would help them feel safe.

At the office, Melanie, Stacy, Tyler and Brianna were there. Stacy was making coffee in a large urn and heating hot water in another.

"Oh Gina, I'm so relieved you're here," said Brianna.

"Thanks, glad I could help."

Melanie said, "Since I'm the oldest I get to be in charge, for once in my ancient life. One group will be here at 9:30. The other at 1:30. Lunch is at 12:30. If there's no customers. If there are, then squeeze lunch in when you can. If you can't, call Brianna in from the greenhouse to cover your lunch. She'll be filling orders. I don't know how much these groups know about recent events. So, I'll be making an announcement about Delia and Renee. And of course, about the storm yesterday. The Sheriff told us that if there's crime scene tape up in an area, then it's off limits. To everyone. I'll tell the customers that. If you need something from one of those areas, then an officer must accompany you and will get what you point at. Brianna's the most likely person that will happen too. The police are trying to stay out of our way and finish up as soon as possible, but I think we're all relieved to have them around. Any questions?"

"What do you want me to do?" asked Gina.

"You, Tyler and I will move plants until the tour group comes. Stacy will ring the bell so we know when they start arriving."

"Okay," said Gina.

They scattered, Stacy to get the office ready. Brianna to start filling orders.

Melanie said, "Grab a hand cart and follow me.

Gina slipped on her work gloves and took one of the heavy duty two-wheeled carts, pulling across the courtyard after her. Melanie and Tyler did the same thing. They headed towards the mist greenhouse.

Which was a mess.

There was still most of a downed Douglas fir lying across part of the mist greenhouse. The branches had been sawed off and the greenhouse next to it sat empty with the plastic covering torn to shreds. They'd obviously cut the end of the tree that overhung that greenhouse and it had fallen in, taking the plastic with it.

Large parts of the mist greenhouse were empty too, but there were still a lot of plants to move.

The center support had collapsed when the tree fell and someone had cut most of the metal pipe out and removed it. Most of the segment supports had been removed and the remaining plastic was shredded.

"Once we get the plants out of this end, I'll call Brian and he'll come back with a friend and take the rest of the tree out. We've got the other end already emptied. So load up your cart, trying to keep like plants together, preferably with tags. Then take them into the tropical greenhouse and unload. Then repeat," said Melanie.

"Who's Brian?" asked Gina, pulling her cart up to a plant bench. She set her water bottle on the first empty plant bench and began to load the delicate cuttings that had recently graduated from the mist tent.

"He lives just down the road. Yesterday, he dealt with all his downed trees and came over to help. I offered to pay him, but he wouldn't take it. Such a good neighbor."

Gina filled up her cart with about eight flats of individual plants. Then hauled it into the tropical greenhouse. Which was surprisingly empty of tropicals.

Melanie was already unloading her cart.

"Where did all the tropicals go?"

"They're outside, braving the elements. The plastic was shredded. So we emptied the greenhouse, removed the old plastic and Tyler and Stacy put up new plastic. Then we began moving in the plants that need the warmth."

"Will they be okay?" asked Gina.

"If the weather stays warm. It's a little earlier than we would normally move them out, but there's no choice. We've got to protect the future, which is in all these babies, not tropicals. And I talked to Karen last night on the Deputy's phone. She agreed with me about not keeping them. So they're up for sale. Almost all of them. We decided to keep a couple, which I took home last night. One for me, one for Karen."

Gina was almost tempted to buy some of them, but then she'd have to take care of them. Plus her cats viewed houseplants as toys. The only place she kept any were in her studio, where she could lock the cats out when she wasn't around.

She continued working and had moved two cartloads of plants when the bell rang.

"I've gotta go be charming," said Melanie. "The gardens are filled with debris. Nothing to do about it today. If you two can continue with this until I get done with the tour, then I'll let you know when we're back and customers need help."

"Okay," said Gina, continuing to work.

Even now, she knew tonight was going to be an epsom salts bath night.

They worked solidly for two hours and had the greenhouse nearly empty by the time Melanie returned.

"Tour's done, can you come help customers find things?"

"Sure. I need the break."

"Awful hard work, isn't it? I really didn't want to get out of bed this morning. Yesterday we moved so many plants and all the tropicals are in larger pots. They're so heavy."

Gina was relieved to see that the visiting group consisted of thirty people. Not like the hordes that had come from the conference.

Melanie addressed the group, "Things are in a bit of disarray today. The windstorm yesterday took out a couple of our greenhouses, so we've had to move things around. This is our control center here. Grab a box, put your name on it and collect the plants you want here. These maps are mostly accurate. Here in this corner, I've crossed out the greenhouses we've lost, only one of which held sale plants. So if the key says your plant was in that greenhouse, it was either moved or crushed beyond life. I've got a list of where plants were moved to. So if you need help with plants in that greenhouse, I'm the one to ask. Gina can help you with anything else. There's a covered area near the shop to take your box when you're ready to check out. Also in that area are a large number of tropical plants that we've decided to sell. We lost a propagation greenhouse and so the one that housed the tropical plants is where our newly propagated plants had to go. Our loss, your gain. The tropical plants really need to spend the next month inside your house or greenhouse. Then can go outside in the summer and back inside in September. There's some beauties in there. So, shopping is officially open!"

The people scattered. Some obviously going for a particular plant, others starting at the first greenhouse and methodically making their way through them. Other people moved towards the office, to check out the tropical plants. There were several plant benches out in the open graveled area, containing hardy shrubs, trees, vines and perennials that gathered interest as well.

"I haven't actually seen the Sheriff or Deputies anywhere," said Gina.

"They're either spread out in the woods or at the house. They're all over the place."

"Looking for anything in particular?"

"I'm not sure, but I sure hope they find what they need soon. We could use Karen back here. I'm not happy playing manager."

It was then that customers descended with questions.

A long time later, Gina ate her sandwich, yogurt and carrots. She was exhausted, but took the time to peruse the tropical plants. About half of them were gone, bought that morning. Melanie must be relieved. A couple of local folks had wandered in and bought some, too.

The orchid she'd painted was still there. Thirty dollars. A beauty, but she doubted that she'd ever get it to bloom again. Both the gingers and the hibiscus were gone. None of them would have tempted her either. A couple of Brugmansia, taller than she was, sat in the corner. One with fragrant yellow bell-like flowers that were about five inches long. The other had peach colored blossoms. They were night fragrant and would begin to have a scent about four in the afternoon. She loved them, but wouldn't be able to haul them in and out of the house twice a year. The plastic black pots filled with soil probably weighed nearly as much as she did. Too much work.

She put her lunch things back in the car and went to find Melanie. She spotted her by the sales greenhouses.

"Well, back to the mines," Gina said.

Melanie asked, "Are you up to moving more plants?"

"Yes."

The bell rang signaling the next group was arriving.

"Okay, I'll go lead the tour and let you know when I'm back so you can help people find plants."

By the time Melanie returned from leading people around the gardens, Gina and Tyler had emptied the broken mist greenhouse. All the new cuttings were tucked away in the former tropical house. They'd have to be watered a lot until a new misting system could be rigged up, but by then hopefully, they'd be ready to be out in the world. Or they'd be dead from all the moisture leaching from their foliage.

"Oh my, you two have been busy. Thank you, thank you. Can you both go help people find plants. I'll call Brian and maybe he can get that tree out of here, so we can see if there's anything else salvageable."

In the last couple of days irises had begun to open. Some of the peonies were large enough to be blooming and scenting the greenhouses. There were fragrant honeysuckle, Fritillaria and rock garden tulips. The May apples, fancy and plain, had leafed out with their extravagant foliage. Heuchera and Hostas were showing off their leaves as well.

Plants in bloom filled people's boxes. No matter how much people raved about the importance of good foliage, they were suckers for a pretty flower.

This group didn't seem as knowledgeable as the morning group. There were thirty-five people and they were just as passionate as the morning group about what they liked. They kept Gina moving, trying to help them find the plants they were looking for.

An hour into helping people Gina saw three men with large chainsaws walk through the nursery. Then the noise began. It was hard to talk to people, but she was grateful the men were removing the remains of the tree from the greenhouse.

Gina began to move slower as the day wore on, her mind

numb from questions. Her arms, shoulders and back tired from moving plants.

The afternoon group were finally all gone at 4:30. The staff gathered in the store.

Melanie said, "I'm good with closing early today. Any objections? We'll call it a full day. All of us did that, just in a few less hours."

"Let's go home," said Brianna. "I'm almost caught up with orders."

Stacy said, "Who's going to take the money to the bank?"

"Oh geez. Karen's not here. What usually happens with the money."

"Delia used to take it home some nights. They have a safe. She always at least took the money for the morning, to fill the cash register. The rest got deposited."

"Where?" asked Melanie.

"The bank on Main. The only one in town. I think there's a drop box. The deposit slip and everything is in the bag," said Stacy, pointing to the blue bag on the counter by the cash register. She pointed to a green bag. "That's for tomorrow, to put in the cash register."

"Do I need a card or anything, or do I just drop it in the deposit box?"

"The deposit slip is enough," said Stacy. "I always make two copies. The other goes to Margaret."

"Thank goodness we have a bookkeeper!" said Melanie.

"Okay, I'll take the money to the bank and the other bag home with me. Thanks everyone. Great work today. Tomorrow won't be as hectic. We do have some people coming, but no big groups. Maybe the gardens will be fully open. We'll see."

They locked the office and Tyler ran out to close the front gates as the staff drove off.

"Melanie, I think we should go over to the house. Look more closely at Delia's houseplants."

"Why?"

"See if we can find the missing plants over there. Why else would someone have broken into the house?"

"I have no objection to looking. And I have Karen's set of keys," Melanie said, holding up a wad of keys. "But let's drive over to the house," said Melanie, in the near empty parking lot. "I don't want to leave all that money in my truck with no one in the nursery."

"Okay. I'll take my car over too. Not walking back alone, after dark. Not here."

Gina parked behind Melanie in the empty, circular drive. It was made of permeable concrete but had bits of blue and silver glittery material in it that lit the entire thing up like a star field. It was quite lovely. The front walk wove through an elaborate garden and was made of the same material. There were motion detector lights closer to the house that welcomed them. Gina would have liked to linger in the garden in daylight. It was nothing like the woodland native garden in the back of the house.

Gina knocked on the door, noticing large gashes in the door. The deadbolt had been ripped out. It looked as if someone had taken an ax to the door and it opened as she knocked.

No one answered.

Melanie tried six keys before she found the right one.

They opened the door and went into the eerily silent house. It smelled like greasy burgers. Empty bags from the local burger place sat on the coffee table. She couldn't tell if the smell was nauseating or just made her hungrier. Her lunch had been all used up. It was dinner time.

Gina flipped a light switch on.

"Don't do that. What if the Sheriff has got the place staked out."

"Those house plants aren't going to water themselves."

"Right. I'll go find the watering can," said Melanie.

She went towards the kitchen.

Gina went to Delia's office, which was quite large. One interior wall had a huge painting on it of a jungle. The chair and desk sat in front of it, facing out into the room. In the center of the room was a brown leather club chair with a footstool, and a large table covered with books, plant catalogs and papers. The next entire wall was floor to ceiling bookshelves filled with plant books and catalogues. Another wall was windows, including a door that led out onto the back patio. The door had bamboo screens that folded out to cover it.

Another wall had a large window with a window box, filled with plants. Grow lights shone down on exotic succulents. In front of the window and on the floor sat stair-step shelves of plants. That was the window they'd passed by the other day.

Gina walked towards it. Melanie followed her with a gleaming silver watering can that had a long, delicate spout, perfect for reaching difficult places.

Plants were jam packed in the window box and on the shelves.

"See anything that looks like the missing plants?" asked Gina.

"I'm looking," said Melanie.

Gina went to the other side of the plant stand and examined every single plant. Which was difficult, there was so much foliage. Delia obviously had many of the large specimen tropicals over here.

"Can we take these off the plant stand. Just so we can make sure we're not missing anything? I can't even see the plants in the window," she asked.

"Fine with me," said Melanie.

Gina and Melanie began taking plants off the top shelf and worked their way down until it was empty, looking closely at every plant. Then as Gina went to begin removing plants in the window box, she noticed a gap between the shelf and the wall. The plants had been covering that. On the floor still getting light from the grow lights, sat several more plants, hidden from view.

"Let's move this shelf out," she said.

"Why?" asked Melanie.

"You'll see."

Melanie helped pull the shelf out.

There sat the variegated peony with its cut leaf foliage, the hydrangea, budded out and ready to bloom and the strange looking Vietnamese plant. Along with a Podophyllum with remarkable patterns on its leaves and a large variegated vine with huge leaves.

"My, my," said Melanie.

"Are those the missing plants?"

"Yes, they are," said Melanie. She reached out and lifted their pots. "And a little dry at the moment. She picked up the watering can and watered them.

"Why did she put them here?" asked Gina, feeling relieved that the plants were safe and healthy.

"She might have been nervous about all the conference people coming through the nursery and didn't want plants this precious in the greenhouse, even if it was marked as off limits," said Melanie.

"Or whoever murdered her, hid the plants here afterwards," asked Gina.

"Why would they do that? Then they wouldn't have access to them?" asked Melanie.

"True. Unless it was someone who was planning on inheriting or buying the place," said Gina.

"But that might take too long. The plants could die in that time."

"Then they'd just break in and take them again." said Gina. "Or at least one of the plants, maybe all. What should we do with them?"

Melanie said, "Leave them here, then. Hidden. Until this is all settled. Then we'll take them back to the nursery. They need to be propagated. That way they won't be so rare. Once there's a few plants in the trade, we won't have to worry about them dying and just being a memory."

They moved the shelf back in front of the plants and loaded it back up again. Melanie refilled the watering can and watered everything.

"We need to tell the Sheriff," said Gina.

"I'll do it. He'll probably be around tomorrow. If not, I'll call him. You've got paintings to frame."

"I do. I'd almost forgotten."

They turned out the lights, locked up and walked to their cars.

"You don't need me tomorrow, do you?" asked Gina.

"No. I think we'll be okay. It won't be that busy. The big thing was moving all those plants. Tomorrow we'll just be sifting through the rubble of the mist greenhouse, they got the rest of the tree out."

"Good luck with that. I hope you find some survivors."

"So do I. Oh. I still have to go to the bank," said Melanie. "I nearly forgot.

"I'll drive behind you and wait till you're done," said Gina. "Just to be safe."

"Thanks. I feel strange with that much money."

Gina followed Melanie out onto the main road. They drove past her section of town and into the center of town. The bank was a white building that looked sort of like an old house. Melanie parked in the empty lot and went up to the well lit front where there was a cash machine. Gina stopped near the front sidewalk. Melanie dropped the bag in the slot, waved at Gina and got back in her truck., then drove off towards home.

Gina turned around in another parking lot and drove home. Every muscle in her body ached. She fed the complaining cats and nuked some frozen cheese enchiladas for herself while running a hot bath filled with epsom salts.

She ate as quickly as the hot cheese would allow, and got in the bath. Alice sat on the lid of the toilet and told Gina about her day. Meowing about *'how could Gina have been gone for two solid days in a row. Again, after the dreadful last stretch of being gone so much.'*

"Yes, yes. I know. You're terribly put upon. If you're a good cat, I'll pick up some catnip at the store where I go by your truly expensive healthy food, next time I'm there."

Alice allowed as to how *'that would begin to make up for it.'*

"And maybe some treats too."

'That would be quite nice,' Alice said.

"That's as much as you're going to get from me, I'm afraid."

Alice lay down and tucked her paws in, curling her fluffy tail around her and sat, watching the water move.

After her bath, Gina decided she was done for the day.

She climbed into bed and fell asleep after she'd found a space between the two cats hogging the bed.

Gina felt a sense of satisfaction that her hunch about the plants had panned out. Now if only the Sheriff could catch the murderers.

DAY 10 - SUNDAY

The next day Gina checked her messages again. Still nothing from Joanna. Her daughter usually called. She decided to check email, her once a week check in. There she found an email.

Hi Mom,

Got the flights. We'll be flying in Tuesday after work. That night we'll stay up near the airport, cause we'll both be exhausted. We'll get a rental car on Wednesday and drive out to stay with you, if that's still all right. So we'll be able to see your gallery opening. How exciting! Tom's meeting begins on Friday and he'll drive back to Seattle and stay in the hotel there. By then I'll know if you want me out of your hair or want me to stay longer, so we'll play the weekend by ear.

Let me know if all this works for you,

Love,

Joanna

Gina tapped in a reply saying yes, that would be perfect and that she was so looking forward to it.

Oh, what fun! She needed to get the house cleaned up and

fresh linens on the guest room bed. And cut some flowers from the garden. And actually plan a few meals. Especially breakfasts.

But first, she needed to get the rest of those paintings matted and framed. Or just framed. No, she'd done mats of the first five, the second batch should be the same.

Time to get dressed and get to work.

Gina spent the next hour matching up frames to paintings and choosing mat colors. By lunch time she only had one mat done.

The afternoon had better go faster.

She cut some sharp cheddar cheese and lay it on a slice of bread. Put a bit of mayonnaise and stoneground mustard on the other piece of bread, lay that on top and put it all in the grilling machine.

Then got a large glass of water. If it was going to remain this warm, she really should make some sun tea. Tomorrow.

She began to make a list of everything to get done in the next three days.

Gina quickly ate her sandwich and went back to work.

She'd just gotten the first painting and mat into the frame and was checking to make sure it looked good, when her cell phone rang.

"Hello."

"Gina, how are you today?" said Melanie.

"Behind, why?"

"Well, I've got lots of news."

"Okay, I'm going to put you on the speaker so I can keep working."

"Framing things?"

"Yes, and it's slow going."

"So, this morning I went into the mist greenhouse and began seeing what I could salvage. Somehow, when the tree fell on stuff, the tables flipped and collapsed but got propped up enough to shelter some of the plants. They're somewhat mashed, but we've got some survivors I think. And they're the Vietnamese plant, the chua. We really have to find out if it has a latin name, or decide if it's an unknown genus and species."

"Yay!" said Gina.

"So also, David showed up this morning. Back from camping. He kept asking for Karen, not believing she wasn't there. I told the Sheriff he was here. Because not only was he wearing black Nikes, but he's limping. Said there was a rockslide, while he was out hiking and a heavy rock fell on his foot. The Sheriff took him in for questioning."

"So, it's not clear if he's been arrested?"

"Not clear."

"Wow," said Gina. "Did he say why he wanted to talk to Karen?"

"No, I gave him every chance. I told him if it was really important that he could ask the Sheriff to dial the Deputy she was with and then he could talk to her that way. He balked at that."

"And you told the Sheriff that?"

"Yep."

"Good. And you told the Sheriff about the plants?"

"Yep. He was ecstatic. But annoyed that we went in there by ourselves."

"There was no crime scene tape or anything."

"No, there wasn't and I told him that. Told him that we just went to water the plants, and that we had to move them all to make sure we weren't missing anything."

"Good. Was it busy today?"

"Not really. Maybe a dozen people all day. Nothing Tyler and David couldn't handle. Well, David didn't really do much of anything. He just looked sullen all day. Even if he isn't a murderer or didn't attack Karen, he's going to be fired. He hasn't been here any day he's been needed. Slacker."

"I sure hope this shakes things loose and David confesses and the other two are caught."

"Me too. I've had enough excitement. I'm ready for life to get back to normal," said Melanie.

"Did you talk to Karen? Tell her about the missing plants?"

"I did, she's over the moon."

Gina was wrestling with one of the frames, trying to pull the backing loose. She needed a screwdriver.

She picked up the phone and went into the laundry room, which was where all the tools were store. Gina dug around with one hand until she found one the right size. She noticed the rather large bin of dirty clothes, much of it covered with mud from the nursery. Another thing to add to the list.

She continued to listen to Melanie talk about the comings and goings of the Sheriff and Deputies. They'd been in every tool shed out in the gardens, taking prints.

Gina sat the phone down and began trying to pry the backing of the frame loose.

"So what were they looking for?" asked Gina.

"Don't know for sure, my guess would be prints that would link someone to Renee's murder. The spade that she was killed with came from one of the garden tool sheds."

"I thought they'd done that when they were there right after she was killed."

"I don't know. Like I said, it was just a guess. Well, I'd better get back to work. Just thought I'd fill you in."

"Thanks, I appreciate it. Oh, Joanna and Tom are coming on Wednesday. They'll get to come to the show."

"Wonderful, I look forward to meeting them. Maybe we could go out to eat while they're here."

"That would be fun. I'll see what they're up for and call you. Tom goes to Seattle on Friday for a meeting all weekend long. Joanna might stay out here."

"Have you told her about the murders?"

"No. It's not like I'm planning on keeping it a secret from her. But we've only had the one short phone call and an email exchange, so it wasn't really the right time."

"Maybe by the time you tell her, everything will be over."

"I sure hope so. It would be good if Karen was able to come back and you could give her job back to her."

"Absolutely. Although I think she's going to need to hire a manager. And it won't be me. Been there, done that."

Gina laughed.

"Okay, I really do have to get back to work now. A carload of people just arrived."

"Okay, bye," said Gina.

She continued to work till diner time. Then ate quickly while catching up on her mail and the newspaper. A bowl of canned chicken noodle soup. Which was passable, not as good as she used to make back in the days when she still cooked.

Two more paintings matted and framed. After dinner she put on latex gloves and rubbed some dark brown acrylic paint onto the gold frame. Letting the paint stay in the depths of the carved flowers and fronds, she polished off the places she wanted highlighted with a rag, until she was satisfied. Then set it on a shelf to fully dry.

It had been a good day's work. Three more paintings ready, two to go. She could finish those tomorrow. Then Wednesday was the hanging for the gallery show. So she'd take the paintings over on Tuesday.

She'd do her grocery shopping after that. Which meant she needed to plan meals tonight or tomorrow. Definitely tomorrow. Tonight, she'd tackle laundry.

Gina put a load in the washer and then stripped the bed in the guest room. She put the blanket and bedspread in the dryer to de-dust them. They weren't dirty, just dusty from not being used.

The sheets went in the laundry basket. She dusted the guest

room and then did a quick dusting of the entire house. Vacuuming would also need to happen tomorrow.

By the time she rolled into bed it felt like she'd done two days worth of work.

She didn't hear from Melanie or the Sheriff. She hadn't expected a call, but still felt uneasy with murderers on the loose.

DAY 11 - MONDAY

Gina woke to her phone ringing. By the time she made it out from under both cats and to the kitchen, it had stopped. Then her voicemail pinged.

"Gina, this is Sheriff Jansson. Please pick up. I know this is your cell phone number. So please tell me you're all right, or I'll be over in about five minutes."

She called him back.

"Sheriff Jansson here."

"Hello, it's Gina."

"Oh good, you're all right?"

"Yes, I just had to fight the comforter and the cats to get out of bed."

"I'm sorry, I had you pegged as an early riser."

"I am. What time is it?"

"Nine."

"Nine? Yikes. I guess I needed the sleep, I've been working too hard. The cats usually wake me up, yowling for food."

He laughed.

"I just wanted you to know that we've arrested David. He's

confessed to attacking Karen. Nothing else yet, but I feel like there's more coming."

"Good. Well, at least that's one down."

"Yes, but it will make any other suspects edgy, when or if they find out. I want to make sure you and Melanie are safe."

"Well, I'm at home all day today."

"Door's locked?"

"Always."

"And tomorrow?"

"Tomorrow I need to take my paintings to the gallery and pick up some groceries. My daughter and her husband are coming on Wednesday."

"I'm going to send a Deputy over. I'd just feel better."

"Do you really think I'm at risk? What would anyone want with me?"

"It won't have escaped them that someone in the nursery has informed on David."

"So you're also guarding Tyler, Brianna and Stacy?"

"We've warned them all. Tyler and Stacy both live with their parents and siblings. In both cases, several hulking older brothers. Brianna lives with her husband and two very large, vocal dogs. You and Melanie both live alone. And I think you're both higher risk."

"Okay," Gina said.

"And you're not going to pull any stunts like the one last night again, are you."

She noticed it wasn't a question.

"We just felt we needed to water Delia's plants."

"Yes, but you also knew the house had been broken into. It's a good thing my Deputy recognized your cars and didn't shoot you. Or arrest you."

"You had a Deputy there?"

"Of course. I was counting on the murderers returning, because they haven't found what they're looking for yet."

"Oh."

"So if you need to go anywhere near the house, or the nursery after or before open hours, please call and let us know."

"I don't foresee that happening."

"Good, I'll keep in touch with you about any arrests we make."

"Thanks," she said. "I appreciate that."

After she hung up, Gina washed her face with cold water, trying to wake up. She felt groggy.

It struck her that she hadn't asked why David attacked Karen. She needed to remember to ask the Sheriff.

Then she fed the cats and got dressed. By then, Deputy Hammond knocked on her door.

"Hello ma'am. I just wanted you to know I was here."

"Please call me Gina. I'm about to make some coffee. Would you like some?"

"That would be wonderful," she said, tipping the rain off her brimmed hat and onto the garden bed near the door. "I haven't had enough this morning."

"I'll bring it out, unless you want to come in."

"I need to stay out here."

"Okay," said Gina.

Inside she got the coffee going and decided on cereal for breakfast. She'd have to hurry in order to get everything done.

After breakfast, she matted and framed the last two paintings. At the last moment, she decided to add a dusky rose color to the gold frame. She rubbed that accent in delicately, taking care not to get any on the painting. Then left it to dry.

Done with that, she cleaned up her studio and put tools away.

Gina made two grilled tuna sandwiches for lunch, and gave one to Deputy Hammond, who insisted that Gina didn't need to feed her, but happily ate it anyway.

After lunch Gina tackled the to do list, planning meals for the next several days and making a grocery list. She figured they would go out to eat some of those days, but it wouldn't hurt to have extra food on hand.

She finished all the laundry. Then vacuumed. Which sent both cats scurrying. Albert went up on top of the refrigerator, staring distrustfully at the vacuum and dusting the top of the fridge with his tail at the same time. Alice hid beneath the bed, so Gina vacuumed the bedroom as fast as she could, then closed the bedroom door to spare the poor cat from the noise.

The house clean, it was time to pick some flowers. She told the Deputy she was going out back and then closed and locked the front door again.

Then with garden scissors and a basket, Gina walked outside to see what she could find. The Deputy came through the gate from the front and stood watching, both front and back.

The lilac bush was still in bloom, so she cut several sprigs of those. She loved the scent.

She was picking for three bouquets. One for the guest room, one for the dining room table and another small one for the bathroom.

On a whim, she cut a couple more lilac sprigs for her bedroom, too.

There were Iris in bloom, so she added those to the basket. And dame's rocket, which would smell sweet in the evening. The Heuchera flowers were long with tiny flowers, which would make a nice accent. She added some Scilla, foxgloves and branches from the tall Fuchsia that had small, light pink flowers dangling from them. The bleeding hearts were still in bloom, but she left those. It wouldn't do to take all the flowers inside. She wanted the garden to look pretty, too.

What she had would be enough. She waved at the Deputy and went back inside, locking the back door.

Then arranged the flowers into four bouquets and set the vases in the appropriate rooms.

There, the house was perfect.

A nice mixture of lived in and beautiful.

Alice and Albert had returned to their favorite places in the living room and were nicely decorative.

Everywhere she went in the house, the scent of lilacs followed her.

It was now five. Time for dinner.

She opened the freezer and perused the selection. Paneer with curried peas and rice it was.

Gina was in the middle of microwaving it when there was a knock on the front door.

It was the Sheriff.

"Just thought I'd let you know there's a change of the guard," he said.

"Who?" she asked, looking around.

"Me."

"You, but surely."

"I'm too old?"

"No, too important."

"Naw. Comes with the territory. I sent the young guy to Melanie's. He's stronger and in better shape. You're stuck with me, since I think you're in less danger."

The microwave pinged.

"I'll let you get back to your dinner," he said.

"Do you want to come in?" she asked.

"No, I'll be out here, just watching. I'm not expecting trouble. Just want to be around if there is."

"Okay," she said. "Did David say why he attacked Karen?"

"Not yet. I'm not done interrogating him. I'm letting him stew a bit."

Gina went inside and set the paper microwave container on a plate, since it was hot.

She carried it over to the dining room table by the window.

The sun was beginning its descent and the clouds were lit up in colors of salmon, purple and a lovely blue gray. She loved this view with its spectacular sunsets.

The curry was just hot enough to complement the buttery flavor of the paneer, an Indian cheese. She loved it and had even made the cheese, back in the days when she was into cooking experiments.

That was before she'd fallen in love with painting plants. After that there had been no looking back. She'd lost interest in a number of hobbies and focused on her painting. Always trying to capture the essence of a plant or flower, to show it off at its best. To tell the observer what she felt and saw in the plant. To show the bud, fruit, the seeds, the dormant season.

Just like life. She'd gone through all those stages in her life again and again. Physically, she might be in the dormant season, but each time she created another painting, the process took her through the entire cycle again.

The attempt at perfection, which of course, was impossible to achieve.

But the attempt was the challenge of it.

Gina cleaned up after dinner and watched a forgettable movie.

Before getting ready for bed, she stuck her head out the front door. The Sheriff was standing there looking out at the street.

"I just thought I'd let you know I'm off to bed."

"Okay, I'll see you in the morning."

"Are you going to be here all night?"

"No, someone else will relieve me in an hour or so. But I'll be back in the morning to follow you around all day."

"When do you sleep?"

He laughed.

"That's not part of the job description."

"But isn't there a union or something?"

"Yes, and there are time rules. I'm following them. Don't worry, I'll get enough sleep."

She went back inside and curled up in bed. It was a good thing she wasn't in law enforcement.

She fell asleep to the scent of lilacs and the purring of cats.

Hoping the murderers would be caught soon.

DAY 12 - TUESDAY

~~~~~~

Gina was dressed and ready to go by nine. The cats were asleep on her bed, so she closed the door, temporarily trapping them inside.

That way she could leave the front door open without worrying about them getting outside.

One of these days, she really should hire someone to build a catio off the back of the house. Then the cats could come and go as they pleased and still be safe from coyotes and the occasional cougar who wandered through.

She took her traveling coffee mug out to the car.

Just as he said, Sheriff Jansson was outside the door.

"Good morning," he said.

"Well hello."

She unlocked her car and set the coffee mug inside.

Then opened the hatch and the two back doors.

Then with two paintings at a time, she brought them out. She'd wrapped each frame and painting in butcher paper to keep it clean and protected. She delicately loaded the two, standing up on the floor of the back seat. Then closed the door.

"Do you need help?" the Sheriff asked.

"No, I'm fine. This is delicate work."

It took six trips, the hatch held four paintings, standing up, she braced them with stacks of blankets and throws on either side of them. The paintings were all safely stowed, strapped or braced in the car.

Inside the house again, she got a light jacket, her purse and then opened the bedroom door. The cats didn't even look up. Slackers.

At the last minute, she grabbed the grocery list. Couldn't leave without that.

Outside she said to the Sheriff, "The first stop is the Mason Gallery. I'll unload everything to have them ready for tomorrow's hanging."

He got in his SUV and followed her across town. She pulled up to a front parking space and got out.

Then got out two paintings and carried them to the door, pushing her way in through the heavy glass.

A man was vacuuming the wood floor of the gallery. He turned it off when he saw her come in.

The gallery was simple. The main room took up two-thirds of the building. It was one large room with the walls and ceiling painted a subtle off white. Today it smelled of the subtle scent of late tulips, arranged in vases in five places around the room. Their green and pink blooms stood out in the nearly white room.

The building consisted of one bathroom, plus a small back workroom where artwork could be stored, coffee and tea made for openings, and bookkeeping got done. Also, sold artwork was wrapped for transport there. Platters of extra food for openings could be stored until needed.

"Good morning, Gina," said Geoffrey Mason.

He was a slender man in his forties. He'd spent several years teaching art history at the university. Then Geoffrey inherited money and moved to Ravens Island, opening the gallery.

"Hello. You said I could bring my paintings in early," she said.

"Absolutely. Why don't you put them over here? Prop them up against the wall." He took one from her and leaned it against a white wall.

She did the same and he helped her bring in the other paintings.

"This is my favorite time you know. When artists deliver their work. It's like Christmas, opening all these wonderful packages," he said. "You never know what's inside."

"But don't you just get socks or underwear, sometimes?" she asked.

"We all need socks and underwear sometimes."

"True."

"What's with the police escort."

"It's all to do with the murders at Ravenswood Nursery."

"Oh, I heard about that. Terrible business."

"Yes, it was."

"The Sheriff thinks you're at risk?"

"Apparently. I don't really see it myself, but I'm not arguing."

"Good. I hope it's all cleared up soon," he said.

"Me too."

When her car was empty, she said, "I'll see you at nine tomorrow."

"Perfect. I don't think the others will be coming until later."

"This is going to be so fun."

"I can hardly wait to see what you've brought," he said.

"You can unwrap them if you want," she said.

"No, I'm going to wait until tomorrow. The anticipation is sometimes the most fun part," he said.

"You were one of those kids who never unwrapped Christmas presents early."

"You're right."

She waved goodbye. Then went to the Sheriff's SUV.

"Next stop is Corr's Grocery. Maybe the only other stop. We'll see if I can get everything I need there."

"Lead on," he said.

At the grocery store, Gina ran through her list, the Sheriff following her. The grocery store was crowded for a Tuesday morning. What was going on? Didn't any of these people work?

She chose a small cart, just so she could get around easier.

She couldn't find the ham she wanted, they were out. So she decided on bacon for the quiche.

It had been a long time since she'd bought so many fresh vegetables. It had been a long time since she'd cooked.

Her life had changed so much with Ewan's death. Both good and bad.

The Sheriff said, "Do you usually buy this much food?"

"No, but my daughter and son-in-law are coming tomorrow, to stay for a few days. Gotta make sure there's food in the house."

"Oh, that's right. How long are they staying?"

"Tom's leaving on Friday. He has a meeting in Seattle all weekend. Joanna might go with him or she might stay the weekend and I'll probably drive her into Seattle, whenever she needs to be there. That part's up in the air right now."

"So, they'll get to go to your gallery opening."

"Yes, I couldn't be more delighted."

"It looks like you're buying enough food to feed an army, though," he said, looking down at her overflowing grocery cart.

Not only had she picked up ingredients for the recipes she might cook, for five days, even though they'd probably go out for one or two of those evenings, but she'd also grabbed several snack foods that Joanna used to like. Cookies and chips and cheeses.

"It's probably too much," she said, "but I'd hate to run out of food."

"And you're too far away to make a trip to the grocery store," he laughed.

"Much, much too far away," Gina smiled.

"Is your family Irish?"

"Part."

"My grandmother was Irish. She was always terrified that there wouldn't be enough food for everyone. Not being a good host was one of the worst things for her."

"I don't know what side I got that from, but yes."

She finished shopping and then checked out. It took six bags for all her groceries. She hadn't bought that much food in years.

At home, the Sheriff insisted on helping her unload the car. She shut the non-moving cats in the bedroom again, while they brought bags inside.

Once they were finished, he called a Deputy, so he could be relieved.

She opened the door so the cats could come out. Albert, the most sociable cat, wandered out to the kitchen and rubbed around Sheriff Jansson's legs while he talked on the phone.

Gina put all the refrigerated things away first. And a bottle of white wine.

The Sheriff finished his phone call and said, "Deputy Hofsteader will be here soon."

"Are you going home to sleep?"

"No, I'm going to have another run at David. See if he's willing to give his accomplices up yet."

"Oh, I hope he does."

"So do I. It would make my life easier."

"Is Mark Morris still in the country?"

"He's in Seattle, touring gardens. For a short while longer. His flight reservation is still a week away."

"Do you think he's in on this?"

"I think there are at least one or two people other than David. I just need solid proof who."

"All that searching you did around Ravenswood, didn't that turn up anything."

"The forensics on that are still out. The labs are backed up with work. We'll see."

There was a knock at the door and the Sheriff opened it. It was the Deputy.

"Well, I'm off, are you here for the rest of the day?"

"Yes, tomorrow I'm going back to the gallery to help hang paintings. Starting at nine."

"They make you hang your own paintings?" he asked.

"No, they allow us to stand around and tell them where to hang them."

"Oh, well that's nice then."

"Yes, it is. That way we can control which paintings go next to the others and how they're grouped. It's a privilege that some galleries don't give artists, or so I hear. Geoffrey is so nice to work with."

"Okay, well, I'll be in touch."

"Hope you get some sleep."

"I'm doing fine. I'll get some this afternoon."

After lunch, Gina settled in with her lists and planning out what needed, or could, be prepared ahead of time. So, she could spend more time with her family.

She made the quiche dough and refrigerated it, letting it rest, before rolling it out.

She did love the feeling of working with dough, the sliding of the rolling pin, then adding more flour to the pin. Turning the dough on the floured surface. Rolling again. It was a nice rhythm. Comforting.

She folded the dough in half, picked it up and draped it over the quiche pan. Then smooshed it into the bottom and sides. Pinching off the crust at the top and throwing the excess away.

Gina set the crust aside and turned the oven on. Then mixed up the filling. Cutting the raw bacon into small pieces with kitchen shears, and dropping the bits onto the crust. Mixing up the eggs, milk, salt, pepper, basil and oregano. Then grating cheese and adding that to the egg mixture. It needed something else. Mushrooms.

She got some out, washed, sliced and sauteed them in butter and added that to the quiche crust. Poured the egg mixture over. It was nice and full.

She carefully put it into the oven to bake. And actually remembered to set the timer.

One meal done. That would be for tomorrow evening.

Thursday evening, they could dine at the opening. Geoffrey always had things so nicely catered.

Then she rinsed off the whole chicken and dried it. She slipped outside the back door, picking some rosemary and thyme just out the back door, next to the patio.

Back inside she put the herbs just under the chicken skin in a few places. Then salted and peppered it and set it in a glass pan, covering it with plastic and stuck it in the refrigerator. It was ready for Friday. Or Saturday. She'd just need to cook up some potatoes to mash and roast the chicken. And make some gravy after it was finished roasting.

Soon, it was dinnertime before she knew it.

Another frozen dinner. She decided on a frozen pizza this time. One topped with mozzarella, fresh tomatoes and basil. Even though the freshly baked quiche smelled delicious. That was for company.

She took a shower before bed and watched another forgettable movie. About a dysfunctional family with a controlling mother. Which wasn't her. She'd managed to escape that one, probably erring on the side of not giving the girls enough guidance. She'd allowed them to fail, more than once, even when she'd seen the fall coming.

She slept badly and had nightmares. There were murders and plants involved.

DAY 13 - WEDNESDAY

Melanie called at eight. Just after Gina got up, fed the cats and was sitting down with her first cup of coffee.

"What's up?" asked Gina.

"The Sheriff's here, at my house. He told me they just arrested Mark Morris at Seatac. And there's no bail, cause he's a flight risk."

"Wow. Does he think he's got all the murderers?"

"I don't know. I do know the Sheriff hasn't talked to him yet. Some other police department did the arresting. I don't know which one. It's complicated because Mark's English. Anyway, thought you'd like to know."

"Let me know when everybody's locked up, I'll breathe easier."

"I'll do that."

"Are you working today?"

"Yes, I'm working nearly everyday. Until Karen comes back. We might close tomorrow though. Brianna's almost caught up on mail order and we're all pooped. If we can finish up watering today, we will. All of us need a day off. This has been so stressful for everyone."

"You can say that again."

"Aren't you hanging the show today."

"Yup. I'm leaving soon. As soon as I can pry my eyes open."

"Okay, well, I'll let you go."

"Hope you get all the watering done."

"We're going to try."

Gina rubbed her face. She was tired. She really needed a day of doing nothing, too. That wasn't likely until next week. There wasn't a lot to do today, though.

She'd told Joanna to text her when they drove over the bridge to the island. She'd either direct them to her house or the gallery.

The house was clean, the dinner was ready, except for making a green salad and warming up the quiche. There was wine for dinner.

Sun tea, that's what she'd forgotten.

She pulled a bunch of tea bags out of boxes and stuffed them into the large two gallon jar and ran hot water inside it. Then set it out on the back patio where the sun would heat it up. When she got home it should be ready to refrigerate so they could drink it tomorrow.

Gina got dressed and left, followed by Deputy Hammond.

Geoffrey was there to open the door for her. Another man, Kevin, wore a tool belt around his hips and was obviously doing the actual work.

The Deputy came in and stood just inside the big glass doors.

Gina began unwrapping the butcher paper around the paintings.

"Oh my, that is simply divine," said Geoffrey, about the orchid.

When she'd unwrapped them all and they stood in a row along the bottom of the stark walls, it was clear to her which paintings looked best together. She began to move them around and then asked, "How much space do I have?"

Geoffrey point to sections of the wall, "I can give you from here, to here."

She began to point out which paintings should go where.

"I think your painting choices are right, but do you really want to put the one in the textured white frame next to the gold frame?" asked Geoffrey. "I think they'd be better separated. Otherwise, the frames clash and it takes attention away from the paintings."

He was right of course. She wasn't taking in the whole effect.

It took two hours to get everything right and most of the paintings hung. By then other artists were beginning to trickle in. She hugged and said hello to two of them, who she already knew.

Then Joanna texted.

Gina replied, *'Almost done here, but not quite. You better come to the gallery.'* She texted directions.

Gina was given some adhesive, to attach to the back of her tags, for the paintings already up and she was working on that as Joanna and Tom came in the door.

She ran to hug them.

"Oh, it's so good to see you both."

Tom was still tall and on the gaunt side. Joanna had lost weight and looked sleek and elegant, her blond hair cut in a bob that looked absolutely flawless.

"You both look wonderful," Gina said.

"Mom, I don't think I've ever seen you in jeans."

"Really, well it's a work day. I wear them quite a lot."

"There are a lot of people here," said Tom, returning her hug.

"The show is having ten artists."

"Ten, very impressive. I think I'll wander and look at things," he said. "It'll be fun to see it now and then again when everything's up."

"I better get these tags up," said Gina. "How was traffic?"

"Awful. It just keeps getting worse and worse in Seattle, doesn't it?"

"Yes. Many of my friends fly out of Bellingham, just to avoid going through Seattle."

"I'll keep that in mind for the future. Although, for this trip Tom will be ending in Seattle."

"Good point." Gina was waiting for Kevin to finish hanging her last two paintings. She was relieved to have come so early. Some of the artists were hanging their own work, but it was clear that Kevin would be in much demand.

Geoffrey and another artist were rolling out what looked like heavy, square white pillars. They came up to her waist. The men were placing the pillars throughout the center of the room. Probably for sculptures.

"These are absolutely gorgeous," said Joanna, about her paintings. "I'm going to have to buy one."

"You don't have to."

"I want to. Do you have any idea how excited I am to have an artist for my mother?" Joanna had her arm around Gina's shoulder and squeezed her. It felt nice to have her daughter proud of her.

"No, I guess I don't. I don't really consider myself an artist. I just paint."

"That's what artists do. Or they sculpt, or take photographs. It's so amazing for those of us who have no talent at that sort of thing."

"Do you know when I started?"

"No, I don't."

"After all of you girls left home. I began taking beginning painting classes and botanical illustration classes. I hadn't touched a paintbrush since I was probably twelve. It's not a matter of talent. It's a matter of learning and practice."

"So you're saying that if I took classes and practiced, I could paint?"

"Yes. If you wanted to badly enough. Not many people do. I didn't think I did, but it gradually took over my life. And your father was making more than enough money for both of us. So eventually, I retired from work. And then there was more time to paint. So I did. And I got better and better."

Gina watched as Kevin hung another painting, taking a level to make sure it was straight. Then he began to make a hole for the last one.

"But your paintings are stunning. I couldn't do that."

"It's taken over fifteen years of almost daily practice to paint like this."

"That long? That's a lot of paintings."

"Yes. But it's just like you, you've been out of school for fifteen years. Learning your trade, honing your skills, learning, taking seminars and doing the work. You're good at it. I know, because you keep getting promoted. But it took fifteen years. I couldn't just walk in and do your work either."

"Good point," said Joanna. "Still, I'd like to find something else to do in my life. I love my work, but it's not enough."

Kevin hung her last painting, checked it was level, nodded at her and went to ask Geoffrey who was next.

"It never is. We humans are complex creatures," said Gina, putting the description/price tags up on the last two paintings. She especially liked the rose that she'd finished from the photographs that day. Gina put a sold tag on it, since Melanie wanted it.

"So, what should I do? I have no time."

"There's never any time. Not when you have a demanding job. You have to steal it, fifteen minutes at a time. Find something you love to do. Doesn't matter what it is. Schedule fifteen minutes a day for it. More time if you can find it. Baby steps."

"Okay. But I don't really know where to begin," said Joanna. "I'm not good at having fun anymore. Neither is Tom. We both lost that knack with having to work all the time."

"I didn't say it would be easy. Make a list of things you used to love to do. As a kid. Keep adding to the list over a few weeks. Put down anything you've ever want to do. Dreaming is something we tend to lose as we age. Don't let it slip away. That's where fun and hope lie."

Tom returned to them. "This is really fascinating. Everyone's art is so different."

"Yes, we all see the world from unique perspectives. I think I'm done here. Just let me check with Geoffrey and see if he needs anything else from me."

Geoffrey was finished moving columns and was walking around the gallery, chatting with people.

"I think I'm done," said Gina. "Do you want to take a look before I leave?"

"Oh yes," he said.

They walked over and Geoffrey said, "That is simply perfect. And your tags are so nice. I didn't know you did calligraphy."

"It's all part of the botanical illustration training," she said. "I'm glad you like it. I was hoping it wasn't too fussy."

"It's perfect for your paintings. I think you're done here. I'll see you tomorrow at just before five then."

"I'll be here," she said.

Gina got her purse and then realized that she didn't quite know how to tell Joanna about the murders and that Deputy Hammond would be following them.

"Shall we go out for lunch?" asked Gina.

"That would be perfect," said Joanna.

"What are you in the mood for?"

"Seafood," said Tom. "Back east, the seafood just isn't as good."

"The Marina has the best seafood in town."

"Great, we'll follow you," said Joanna.

"If you want, you can leave the rental car here and we can pick it up after lunch. It's safe here."

"I'd like a break from driving," said Tom.

"Great, I'll drive then." As they followed her out the door, she clicked the Prius open and said, "The blue Prius is mine."

Tom and Joanna walked towards it.

Gina lingered to tell the Deputy where they were going.

Deputy Hammond nodded and said, "I'll come in and look around, then wait out in the parking lot and do an occasional check-in. You have my number to call or text if there's trouble, right?"

"Yes, I do."

"Good if someone looks suspicious, or if you're simply not feeling safe, call me. Please don't hesitate."

"I will."

Gina got in the car and drove to the Marina.

It wasn't crowded. Only half a dozen tables having a late lunch.

She ordered a fish sandwich, with halibut, and iced tea. Tom decided on the oysters and a pale ale, and Joanna, grilled salmon and iced tea.

After the server left, Gina told them about the last couple of weeks. They were horrified that she'd been working at the nursery where murders had taken place.

"That explains the police who followed us from the gallery," said Tom.

"Yes. She's been following me for the last couple of days. Just in case."

"And at home, too?" asked Joanna.

"Yes."

"They must be worried if they're guarding you day and night," said Tom.

"They're doing the same for Melanie. They're worried because we live alone. And we actually found the plants, and overheard some of the suspects talking about their future plans."

"How many of them are still on the loose?" asked Joanna.

"They think one."

"They think?" asked Tom, raising his eyebrows at her.

"I haven't talked to the Sheriff today. I don't know what he knows and what he doesn't."

"Mom, I don't like this at all. They're putting you at risk."

"Joanna, this is a small island. There's a Sheriff and possibly three Deputies. Two of them are guarding Melanie and myself, day and night. The other two are still investigating, interrogating and guarding the crime scenes. None of them are sleeping much. They've had to pull in other departments from the next county over. I really don't think the other murderer is going to come after either Melanie or I, but the Sheriff is doing everything possible to keep us safe, if that should happen."

"Your mom's right," said Tom. "Our police force wouldn't do nearly as much."

"But, she's my mom."

"And she's not helpless."

"I should hope not," said Gina.

"Do they know who the other suspect is?" asked Joanna.

"I don't know. Last time I talked to the Sheriff, they were still interrogating people."

Their food came and brought an end to that conversation. Which made Gina feel relieved. She didn't want Joanna, or Tom, to worry. And she was pleased Misty wasn't working. Otherwise the news would be all over town, like a windstorm.

The fish in her sandwich was soft and perfectly cooked. Just the way she loved it, with the Marina's perfectly balanced tartar sauce. The iced tea was strong and lemony.

"I feel like I've gone to heaven," said Tom, after sliding an oyster down his throat and following it with a sip of ale.

"They have very good beer here. So many choices," said Gina.

"You like beer?" asked Tom.

"Yes, although my taste runs to the darker, maltier ales."

"Since when do you like beer?" asked Joanna.

"Well, there's been a revolution here in microbreweries. It's not just the huge companies with their cold, thin bitter stuff. I hate that. It's not beer. Now there's so many choices and each season, brings out new ones."

"I've been reading about how the beer industry has been growing so fast in the last decade," said Tom. "In the Northwest, it's gone completely insane."

"Sort of like espresso stands and coffee shops," said Gina.

"Interesting," said Joanna.

Gina said, "I remember there used to be a local comedy show. They had a running skit about the last corner in Seattle that didn't have an espresso stand. That was over twenty years ago."

They finished lunch, then drove back to the gallery, where Joanna and Tom got the rental car. Joanna drove, following Gina home. Trailed by the Deputy.

At home, they parked next to her in the carport.

Both Alice and Albert came out to greet them.

Gina got them ensconced in the guest room and checked her messages. There were none.

After dinner, Melanie called.

"Gina, are you okay?"

"Yes, why?"

"I'm not. While I was at work today, my place was broken into."

"Oh no. Was anything taken?"

"No. The Deputy thinks they might have been looking for the plants."

"Is the house still being guarded?"

"Yes. And so is the nursery. But what creeps me out is that they know where I live."

"That is creepy. They must have followed you home one day."

"Yeah. I'm so glad Deputy Hofsteader's here. He's young and burly, sort of. Makes me feel safer."

"Good. Is your place torn up?"

"No. The door's broken out around the deadbolt. Someone must have taken a sledgehammer to it."

"Really, wouldn't the window be easier?"

"Maybe, but that's what they did at Delia's too, remember how the door was all busted up."

"Yes. So you'll have to get a new one."

"Tomorrow. We decided to close the nursery tomorrow. Give everyone a much needed day off. Maisie and Flopsy are a bit freaked out too. They're just getting used to their new home and someone comes busting in. They were hiding under the bed when I got home. Took an hour to get them out. And that was only with cat food."

"Poor cats. I'm so sorry. Are you staying there tonight?"

"Yes. I'm not leaving home, unless someone stays here to guard it. But obviously they didn't find the plants here, so they left."

"They, being who?"

"Probably Erickman. Although the Sheriff's being a little tight with information at the moment. He came and went. Said he had to make sure to tell all the others. I suppose the Sheriff will drop by your house, but he was worried about Brianna, Stacy and Tyler since they aren't being guarded."

"Of course," said Gina.

After Joanna and Tom got settled in, they came back out of the guest room.

"So, this house is small, compared to the one I grew up in, on Capital Hill. Where do you paint?" asked Joanna.

So Gina showed them her studio, overlooking the bay, with windows covering most of one wall and a large window in the other exterior wall.

"It's beautiful," said Joanna.

"It's a bit messy," Gina said, picking up her watercolor pad and leaning it against a shelf before Alice could stand on it. "I lock the cats out, because they would love to cause mischief in here when I'm not around. So any chance they get to come in, they take.

Albert was exploring beneath her worktable. Alice was on top of it, batting at scissors and pencils, looking for something that moved on its own, like a spider or fly.

"You, you wouldn't cause trouble, would you?" Joanna asked Alice, petting her.

Alice meowed.

"But you don't do all of your painting here," said Tom. "Not if you were painting up at the nursery."

"No. Here I paint plants or flowers I've brought inside. Or sometimes from photographs. But it's always fun to go paint in someone's garden or greenhouse too. I was painting tropical plants in one of the greenhouses there because it's so early in the season. I was trying to get a lot of flowers done for the show tomorrow."

"I rather like this one," said Tom, of an unframed painting hanging on a cork board.

"I do too. I painted that Arisaema in a friend's garden last spring. That was just sort of a sketch. The one I made for them was a larger more elaborate painting."

She opened a photo album and showed him a photograph of the painting.

"Oh. I like that one even better. What a strange plant," he said.

"Yes, nature makes some very peculiar flowers. It's relative of our native Jack in the pulpit. Although the one in the painting is from somewhere in Asia. I can't remember where."

"I remember Jack in the pulpits from when I was a kid. I can see the similarity now," he said.

There was a knock on the front door.

"I better answer that," she said. "Just keep an eye on the monsters."

"The monsters?" asked Joanna.

"The furry ones."

"Oh," Joanna said. "Who took my mother away and replaced her with someone else?"

Gina laughed. She hadn't seen Joanna in probably a decade. They'd both changed. Joanna just hadn't expected her to.

The Sheriff was at the door.

"Hello," she said.

"Mind if I come in?" he asked.

"Not at all. My daughter and son-in-law are staying here. For a visit."

"Not locals then?"

"No, East Coast. They're out for a few days."

"Well, I better talk to them as well, then."

"Follow me," she said, walking towards the studio.

She introduced everyone.

"I'm sorry to bring bad news. We've caught two of the murderers. The third one is still on the loose."

"Who?" asked Gina.

"Karl Erickman. I've talked to David, quite a lot and had one chat with Mark Morris. There will be more. Karl told them he was going up to Vancouver with some friends, here from the conference. He hasn't returned to Seattle yet."

"And you think he was at Melanie's today?"

"Yes."

"Won't they catch him at the border?" asked Joanna.

"It's possible. It's also possible that he already went through, before we contacted the border police. Some of his friends were apparently from Bellingham so he could be there. At any rate, he will be caught. Sooner or later."

"Do you know yet who murdered Delia and Renee?"

"Apparently they wanted to make sure each of them were equally guilty, so they wouldn't rat each other out. Mark killed Delia, Karl killed Renee and David was supposed to kill Karen. And that's where things began to fall apart."

"Why Karen?" asked Gina.

"They thought she knew where the plant was."

"Which plant?"

"Well all of them really. They wanted the plants and the nursery. The Vietnamese plant to sell to a drug company and make some fast, easy money. When Delia was trying to bring Mark into the nursery, she had a potential deal with a drug company. They wanted an exclusive deal, no other drug companies could have access or information about the plant. But the three of them also planned on make a lot of money from the other plants, the hydrangea and the peony. And have the status of taking the nursery over and carrying on the good work, as one of you mentioned."

"Wow. So, you don't know where he is right now, or what he's up to?" asked Gina.

"No. We've contacted law enforcement statewide. Like I said, he'll be arrested. We've frozen his accounts. He's not using his cell phone. Mark said they planned to meet tomorrow, so we'll just do what we do best. Wait."

"It must drive you crazy," said Joanna.

"I've learned patience over the years. Only a few criminals are very, very smart. Most of them, especially these three don't have much experience and make stupid mistakes."

"Like what?" asked Tom.

"Trying to attack someone in the same place they've already murdered two people."

"What would you have done?" asked Tom.

"Followed Karen home. David knew she lived alone, except for the dogs. But to attack her when several of her coworkers were at the nursery wasn't terribly bright."

"Neither is calling in sick on one of the busiest days of the season, then going out to eat with your girlfriend in the same town," said Gina.

"No, I do think David was the weak link in their plan," said the Sheriff. "Well, I'd better get outside. Give the Deputy a break. I'll be here till the middle of the night."

"Shall I bring you out a plate of quiche?" Gina asked.

"I'd be happy if you did."

He reached down and petted Albert who'd been winding around the Sheriff's legs, leaving fluffs of white fur on the black pants. Then the Sheriff left the room, Albert trotting along in front. Alice almost flew off the table in the same direction.

"They really like the Sheriff," said Tom.

Gina glanced at the clock and laughed.

"It's an hour before their dinner. They think anyone moving towards the kitchen must be going to feed them."

They shut the studio door and opened up the wine and sat down at the table looking out at the view.

Eventually, cats were fed. The quiche was brought out and heated. Gina washed and dried the salad greens in the spinner. Then chopped up some yellow bell pepper and a tomato, tossing them with the greens. She pulled a couple of bottles out of the refrigerator: sesame tamari salad dressing and poppyseed ranch.

Joanna set the table with plates and silverware. Gina set out the salad dressing and Tom cut the quiche. Gina dished up some salad and put ranch dressing on it. Added a slice of quiche and took it out to the Sheriff.

"Thank you. I don't often get fresh vegetables. Usually it's burgers."

"Can I get you something to drink?"

He pointed to his thermos. "I've got coffee, thanks."

Gina went back inside and sat down at the table.

"I just love your view. This is a perfect size house," said Joanna.

"I love this house. Wish we'd moved out here a couple of decades ago so your father could have enjoyed it more."

Joanna put down her fork.

"I'm sorry I didn't come out for the funeral."

"Don't worry about it. I understand you didn't have a choice. I used to have a similar job, remember? When there's a big project and it's mandated that no one gets time off for any reason and it looks really bad if the head of Human Resources takes time off, even for a funeral. And we all grieve in our own way."

"But I still feel guilty. Not even going to my father's funeral."

"Oh honey, let it go. He wasn't there. His ashes were, but his spirit was long gone. Funerals are for the living, not the dead. We all knew you loved him. You're so much like him."

"I wasn't there for you, either."

"No, but I understood why. Shelly and Trina came. My friends came. I had enough support."

"You're sure?" asked Joanna.

"Absolutely sure."

"Okay, I'll try to set it aside."

"You can't be all things to everyone," said Gina. "You need to be enough for yourself and work your way out from there. There's never enough of any of us to go around to all the places we'd like."

Gina enjoyed dinner and their talked ranged from everyone's work, to travel, to philosophy. It was nearly ten before she started to droop.

"I'd better get to bed. It's been a really busy week. I've got to be fresh for tomorrow."

"Sleep in," said Tom. "I'll get up and feed the cats. And I'll cook pancakes. You can reheat them if they're cold when you get up."

"Really?" said Gina. "I haven't had anyone cook breakfast for me in . . . decades."

"Really," said Tom, firmly. "I don't get to cook breakfast often. We're always rushing off somewhere on weekends."

"Wonderful," she said.

Even so, she didn't sleep well with worrying about Karl Erickman.

DAY 14 - THURSDAY

Gina woke to the sound of someone in her kitchen. She panicked for a moment, then heard Joanna's voice.

Her door was closed. They must have closed it after the cats left to eat breakfast. The closed up room intensified the scent of lilacs on her bedside table.

She stretched and considered rolling over, it was so nice to have the bed to herself. Then glanced at the clock. Ten in the morning. She must have slept eleven hours.

Well, it had been an exhausting couple of weeks.

The sun shone in beneath the curtains. She finally got up and opened the curtains. Her bedroom faced the front of the house, the windows blocked from the street by a rather ostentatious Rhody planted about eight feet away. One of the few on her property. It was currently blooming with peach colored flowers that had yellow and burnt orange throats. Very showy. Which was why she'd kept it. That, and the evergreen foliage which made a nice barrier to the street and the neighbors across the way.

Gina could see an SUV parked in front, which she recognized as the one Deputy Hammond drove.

Gina dressed quickly in jeans, a t-shirt and her crocs. She'd change later for the show. Find something more arty. She ran the brush through her hair. Then pulled the blankets and bedspread over the bed, doing a haphazard job of making it. Fluffs of white, orange and black fur flew through the air. Probably time to wash her own bedding. She'd do it next week. After Joanna left.

She went into the bathroom and washed her face and put on moisturizer. Then went to the kitchen. Which smelled heavenly.

Coffee and pancakes

"Have a seat Mom, I'll get you a cup of coffee."

"Okay, I'm not used to being waited on."

"Yeah, but it's nice occasionally. Enjoy it while you can."

Joanna brought her a cup of coffee and a plate.

Then returned with a stack of hot pancakes and butter. Then Joanna brought peanut butter and syrup.

"I don't remember when I last had pancakes," Gina said.

"I don't have them often either, but sometimes Tom wants to make them."

Gina plated up a couple of pancakes, smeared them with peanut butter and drizzled syrup over the top.

"I remember Dad used to eat them with peanut butter too," said Joanna.

"Yes. It makes sense when you think about it. Some protein to combat all the sugar."

There was a knock at the door. Tom went to answer it.

He took a plate from Deputy Hammond who said, "Can I say this is the best place I've ever guarded? Thanks for breakfast, and all the other food."

"You're welcome," said Tom. "and I'm sure I can say that for all of us."

She went back outside and closed the door.

"Is there anything the two of you want to do today?" asked Gina.

"Not really," said Joanna.

"It would be so nice to have a lazy day just hanging out around here," said Tom. "We've both been traveling so much. Too much. Staying in one town for a couple of days sounds nice. And not having a schedule, other than your opening tonight, is wonderful."

"That's right, you're going to be working all weekend aren't you?"

"Yes. From Friday evening until Sunday afternoon. Although the dinners are going to have Northwest beer and wine, so that'll be a bonus."

"I haven't been home much lately either," said Gina. "The cats have been lonely."

Alice was sitting on the couch, watching all the humans. Albert sat on the back of the couch watching birds out the window and meowing at them.

The day passed quickly with the great conversation, and soon it was time to dress. Gina put on a pair of black pants, flat black shoes and a silky purple, cerise and black top. At the last minute she added some cerise lipstick. And a small black purse, just large enough to hold her phone, keys, some credit cards and cash. Oh, and the lipstick.

Tom wore a classy looking grayish suit with a blue shirt and tie. Joanna wore dressy pale blue pants and a deeper blue blouse that matched her eyes.

Gina fed the cats again.

Then they went out to the car.

Deputy Hammond got in her vehicle to follow them.

At the gallery, nearly all the artists were already there, judging by the number of cars in the side lot. Gina noticed the Sheriff's SUV was parked behind the gallery. Deputy Hammond parked back there too. Out of sight from the road and the main parking lot.

She guessed Karl Erickman was still on the loose.

They got out and went inside.

Gina felt a little anxious and excited. She walked into the center of the gallery and gasped.

"This is all so beautiful."

"Oh hello Gina," said Geoffrey. "Isn't it though. It's like walking into a floral shop. A perfect May day show."

In vases, spread throughout the room, were bouquets of lilacs, peonies and lilies, so the entire gallery smelled like a flower shop, too.

"Here's your name tag," said Geoffrey looping a purple string and tag around her neck. "And do you have any business cards?"

"I don't. I've been meaning to go to a printer in Seattle and get some done. It just hasn't happened."

"How about a website I can point people to?"

"Nope. It's just me. If they want to commission something, you can give them my phone number or email address."

"I expect I'll be doing a lot of that in the near future."

Another artist came in the door and Geoffrey said, "Well, I'd better give Sam his name tag. Circulate. The catering people will be coming out of the back soon. And guests will be arriving soon too."

After he left, Joanna said, "Mom, I can make you a website while I'm here. And teach you how to update it. Then you could put photos of your paintings on it, to sell. And I could help you design business cards and get them printed online. Very inexpensively."

"Really? People would buy paintings off the internet? Sight unseen?"

"Yes. You'd have to know how much shipping would be for the painting. And add that to your price. You could also have an events page and put gallery shows like this up on it."

"And you think I would be able to work it myself?"

"Yes. I do. I can make it simple for you. You'll need to write down my instructions, because you won't be able to remember them. Not many people do."

"Well, that might be fun," said Gina.

"It will," said Joanna.

Melanie was one of the first people in the door.

"Hello," she said, giving Gina a hug and a bouquet of flowers, the stems in a wet paper towel and plastic wrap. There were bleeding hearts, fuchsias, lilacs, lilies, and several other garden flowers she couldn't name.

"Hi," Gina introduced her to Tom and Joanna, then said, "Those aren't from Ravenswood, are they?"

"No, the nursery was closed today. I picked these from my garden, while I was waiting for the guy to bring the new door and install it."

"Did he come?"

"Yes, at three. Finally, but it's all done. So what have you been up to today?"

"Just hanging about. It was lovely. A relaxing day, for the first time in a long while."

"Shall I put these in the car for you?" asked Joanna, about the flowers.

"Yes please. I can't wait to munch on the food. I'm getting hungry."

The gallery was rapidly becoming crowded. The caterers had brought platters of appetizers out to tables set on two sides of the room. They were circulating with trays carrying glasses of wine and water.

Gina chose a glass of red wine and sipped it. It was a brazen wine with lots of complexity. She loved it. She went over to a food table and got some brie and crackers on a small plate and stood looking at some of the paintings while juggling her plate and the wine.

One of the artists had painted a giant canvas, with oil or acrylic. It was a deep, sky blue background fronted by a fluffy pale apricot colored peony. Gina couldn't stop staring at it. She simply loved it. It made her feel the way spring did. New life, new hope.

Geoffrey came up beside her and said, "It's interesting, isn't it?"

Which, being Geoffrey meant the painting was either godawful or spectacular. He couldn't decide.

Gina laughed and said, "I just love it. How much is it?"

"Four hundred. But for you, with an artist's discount, three hundred fifty."

"Sold."

"Oh, really? I didn't expect an artist to be my first sale. Here, take this sticker, write your name on it and stick it on the wall, beneath the tag. I'll put it in my notebook."

He handed her a page of stickers and a pen, and took her empty plate. She followed his instructions, grinning. This would be perfect to replace the landscape in the living room. She'd never liked it. Ewan had loved it. She'd kept it as sort of a memento of him, but didn't need it any more.

Joanna came up to her and asked, "Are you buying this?"

"Yes, I just love it. I can't stop looking at it."

"It's beautiful. It'll fit perfectly in your house. But where?"

"The landscape above the bookshelves is going. I've never liked it."

"I love that painting. I remember it from the old house."

"So did Ewan. I never have. It's yours."

"Really?"

"Swap it for a website."

"Deal," said Joanna, shaking her hand. "I've got just the place for it."

A crush of people came through the front door. Gina noticed the Sheriff standing against the wall, just inside the door and off to the left a bit. He was taller than most people, so he was easy to spot.

"Gina, this is Paul Frost. He's interested in your work," said

Geoffrey, gently pulling her over to the wall of where her paintings were hung.

"Hello," she said, shaking his hand.

"Where did you find such glorious flowers?" he asked.

"I was up at Ravenswood Nursery. The tropical plants are from their greenhouses. Although I think most of them were sold at the end of last week. They lost a greenhouse in the windstorm and had to sell them off. But the others, like this rose and the peony, are from their gardens."

"My, my. I can't tell you how much I love them. We're finishing up a remodel of our entire house. My wife and I. We just moved back in and we've been looking and looking at art. We wanted something both refined, yet on the wild side. I think your work fits perfectly. Do you ever do anything larger?"

"Yes, I have done a few. As commissions. When people wanted paintings to fit larger spaces."

"These are perfect for the dining room, but for the living room, we'd need something larger. Why don't I give you my card? If you'd be so kind as to call next week, we can have you over and you can see the place. Look at our furniture and the way things fit together."

"That would be lovely," said Gina. "Are you looking for particular flowers or plants, or is color more important?"

"I like exotic plants, but my wife is a color person," he said. "She couldn't come tonight, but demanded that I come, after seeing the flyer for the opening. She loved your work. I texted her photographs of the two paintings I told Geoffrey I wanted and she responded that they were stunning. And perfect for our dining room."

"Good. It's nice when people who live together agree."

"Isn't it?" he said. "I'd love to chat further, but I need to leave. So please call."

"I will," she said.

She watched him walk off and then felt a hand grip her right wrist so hard, she nearly cried out.

"Silence," hissed a voice in her ear. "I've got a gun pointed at your side, that will blow a hole in you. You're leaving with me. Now."

Gina felt something hard poke her in the side. Her heart leapt to her throat and she had to force herself to take a breath.

She didn't have to think about who the voice might belong to.

He turned her towards the door and pushed her along in front of him.

She felt helpless. And angry. A mass of confused images.

But she remembered the advice from somewhere, "Never let a kidnapper get you in a car with them."

Sheriff Jansson was still at the door, looking around. And there was only one door. Deputy Hofsteader must be mingling.

How did Erickman plan on getting her out the door?

"Mom, where are you going?" shouted Joanna.

The Sheriff glanced at Joanna and then Gina. He saw Erickman.

At that moment, Gina remembered to stomp on Erickman's foot and she twisted his right arm backwards while moving away from the gun and his left hand. He still had hold of her when the Sheriff and the Deputy collided with him.

Sheriff Janssen wrenched the gun away, while the Deputy kicked Erickman's feet out from under him.

Gina was immediately surrounded by Melanie, Joanna and Tom.

"Are you okay?" asked Joanna.

"My arm hurts, but I'm fine. Thank you."

"I couldn't let him take my mom," said Joanna, hugging her.

When Erickman was hauled to his feet, he wore handcuffs. He'd shaved his head and mustache and wore mirrored sunglasses and a dark suit. Which was possibly why he hadn't been recognized.

Gina barely recognized him. She shivered.

The Sheriff nodded at her and said, "Sorry about the intrusion folks. We'll be leaving now."

He said something to Deputy Hammond, who stood nearby. She took a position just inside the door, but she was grinning.

Then Sheriff and Deputy Hofsteader pulled Erickman out the door.

Geoffrey was looking a bit worried, then his face abruptly changed and he said, "Our police department at work. They do a fine job."

He retreated into the back room and instrumental Celtic music flowed out over the sound system.

Gina saw through the window, both the Sheriff's and Deputy's vehicles drive away.

"Was that the guy, Mom?"

"Yes, it was."

"What guy?" asked Paul Frost.

Melanie was standing nearby and filled Paul in about all the murders and the suspects.

Eventually Geoffrey came over and said, "Well, that went well."

"That was planned?" asked Gina.

"The Sheriff called me earlier today and said, that there might be a problem. He told me they would be here if there was. And they were. I didn't know the particulars."

Melanie didn't tell him and neither did Gina.

Paul Frost just said, "So, these paintings were painted at the Ravenswood Nursery while there were murderers on the loose. My, my. What a story they have behind them. That makes them doubly valuable."

Geoffrey took it from there. An hour later the gossip had made it round the room and all of Gina's paintings had sold. One of them, the Hibiscus, painted while Delia was being murdered, actually had a bidding war going on and the price tripled before everyone bailed out except the buyer.

"I'm glad I bought the rose before the prices went up," said Melanie, grinning.

"I would never have let you pay that much."

"I know, but I've always loved that rose in person. Now I can have it in my bedroom."

A little later, Brianna and her husband Keith came in. Followed by Stacy and Tyler.

"Such beautiful paintings," said Brianna. "You're going to come back in the summer and paint some more, right?"

"Yes, I think I will."

Now that all the murderers were locked up.

But Gina left that part unspoken.

She had another glass of wine and more cheese and crackers. Tonight she was ignoring the vegetables. People came and went and Gina spoke to more of them than she could remember. The artist of the painting she bought, Madeline Barnes, was absolutely thrilled. Gina knew she had many people who collected her work and participated in large gallery shows around the country.

"I'm so flattered that you liked it enough to buy it. I love your work. I didn't get a chance to buy any before they were gone. You're going to be famous you know. Your art is stunning. You take the best of botanic illustration and add to it. Reminds me of Margaret Mee's work. This is the beginning. The murder angle of it, will just build your reputation. You've helped give those women's deaths a meaning, their nursery will recover. The work they did, the plants they grew will also live on in your art. It is uncomfortable, but just let that be and focus on your painting. Let other people work on selling your art by word of mouth."

Gina did feel uncomfortable about that. She didn't want her paintings associated with murder, but it wasn't her choice. She had no control over what people said. In the end, Madeline had a good head for business.

At almost seven, more people came in. Among them, Karen, with another deputy.

"Oh, I'm so glad we made it," said Karen, coming up to her and taking her hands.

"I didn't expect you," said Gina.

"I came the minute the Sheriff called and said it was clear. The dogs are still in the car. I haven't even taken them home. Well, to my rental. But now I have a real home! I can't wait to move in."

"I'm glad you took the time to come, thank you."

"So where are your paintings? Oh, I'd recognize that peony anywhere," said Karen. "They're all sold. I really wanted to buy one."

"There will be more paintings," said Gina. "That is if the new owner of Ravenswood lets me paint there."

"Absolutely," she said, smiling. "You are our resident painter. Although the tropicals will be sadly lacking in the near future."

"I don't much like tropicals, anyway," said Gina. "Actually, I'd rather paint foliage."

"We have lots of that. But I think your flowers will probably sell better. Just like at the nursery."

"True."

The gallery opening was a smashing success. At seven-thirty the reception ended. Gina was exhausted and exhilarated at the same time.

Tom and Joanna had a marvelous time. They had been chatting up the other artists, collecting their cards and Joanna was planning on spending the evening looking at artist's websites.

The nursery would be open tomorrow. Karen was thrilled to be going back to work and reorganizing the things that needed it. And having a talk with the bookkeeper. She wanted to get the damaged greenhouses rebuilt as soon as possible. There was a lot of propagating to be done.

Everyone was relieved the murderers had all been caught and they could get on with their lives.

Gina, Joanna and Tom went back to her house. Gina slipped out of her shoes as soon as she walked in the entry way.

"I didn't remember those shoes being so uncomfortable."

She got out another vase and put the flowers from Melanie in it and set them on the coffee table.

"Those are beautiful," said Joanna. "We're meeting her for dinner tomorrow night, right?"

"Yes. Melanie's my dearest friend."

"And yet, you only met her when you moved here, a couple of years ago."

"Yes. But we just clicked. We have the same tastes, mostly. The same sense of humor. She's much more of a gardener than I am, but that's what she's done as a living for decades. She propagates plants at the nursery. Only part time now."

Joanna had gotten her laptop out and was looking at websites. Tom had taken down the landscape hanging in the living room.

"You're sure this is all right? Me taking it to mail tomorrow? You're going to be looking at a blank wall for a month, till the show's over."

"Yes. Then I won't have to mail it to you. And I'll be able to bring the apricot peony home and put it right up. They're about the same size."

"I think you're right about that."

He brought Gina a glass of sun tea. She was sitting with her feet up and Alice was on her lap.

"She just wants to be here because I'm wearing black pants. It'll show off the clods of fur she leaves behind very nicely."

"She missed you and you know it," said Joanna.

Alice purred in response.

And everything was right with her world.

ABOUT THE AUTHOR

Linda Jordan writes fascinating characters, funny dialogue, and imaginative fiction. She creates both long and short fiction, serious and silly. She believes in the power of healing and transformation, and many of her stories follow those themes.

In a previous lifetime, Linda coordinated the Clarion West Writers' Workshop as well as the Reading Series. She spent four years as Chair of the Board of Directors during Clarion West's formative period. She's also worked as a travel agent, a baker, and a pond plant/fish sales person, you know, the sort of things one does as a writer.

Linda now lives in the rainy wilds of Washington state with her husband, daughter, four cats, seventeen Koi and an infinite number of slugs and snails.

Her other work includes:
~Notes on the Moon People
~Faerie Unraveled: Bones of the Earth Book 1
~Living in the Lower Chakras
~Bibi's Bargain Boutique
All her work can be found at your favorite online bookseller.

Get a FREE ebook!
Sign up for Linda's Serendipitous Newsletter at her website:
www.lindajordan.net

Made in the USA
Columbia, SC
20 August 2019